ECHO
LOCA
TION

STORIES

ECHO LOCA TION

KAREN HOFMANN

NeWest Press

Library and Archives Canada Cataloguing in Publication
Hofmann, Karen Marie, author
Echolocation / Karen Hofmann.
Issued in print and electronic formats.
ISBN 978-1-988732-56-5 (softcover).
ISBN 978-1-988732-57-2 (epub).
ISBN 978-1-988732-58-9 (Kindle)
I. Title.
PS8615.O365E24 2019   C813'.6   C2018-904448-9   C2018-904449-7

Board editor: Anne Nothof
Book design: Natalie Olsen, Kisscut Design
Cover texture © successo images/shutterstock.com
Author photo: Julia Tomkins

NeWest Press acknowledges the Canada Council for the Arts, the Alberta Foundation for the Arts, and the Edmonton Arts Council for support of our publishing program. This project is funded in part by the Government of Canada. ❡ NeWest Press acknowledges that the land on which we operate is Treaty 6 territory and a traditional meeting ground and home for many Indigenous Peoples, including Cree, Saulteaux, Niitsitapi (Blackfoot), Métis, and Nakota Sioux.

#201, 8540–109 Street   Edmonton, Alberta   T6G 1E6
780.432.9427
NeWest Press   www.newestpress.com

No bison were harmed in the making of this book.
Printed and bound in Canada   1 2 3 4 5   21 20 19

To those who go on foot,
and who pay attention to their footing.

CNTENTS

Virtue Prudence Courage **9**

That Ersatz Thing **23**

Vagina Dentata **41**

The Bismarck Little People's Orchestra **55**

Echolocation **65**

The Swift Flight of Data into the Heart **77**

Unbearable Objects **103**

The Canoe **115**

Clearwater **131**

The Burgess Shale **153**

Holy, Holy **159**

The Birds of India **181**

Instant **201**

The Flowers of the Dry Interior **223**

Acknowledgements **253**

VIRTUE
PRUDENCE
COURAGE

HE SAID *dream vandals*, the animals roaming the island at night.

What kinds of animals? she asked. She had never heard a man talk about his dreams before. It was like hearing him say *frightened* or *pussy*. She blushed. She was wearing little suede boots, jeans, a long baggy sweater, jade-green. All of her clothes were cheap. She had pale eyelashes mascara didn't stick to, and an overbite – she had been raised by her grandmother, no dental plan – and tended to hide behind her hair, which was not cut properly, and fell like a hood around her face, thick mats of it slanting across her forehead and over her cheeks.

At this party at her residence, she had been approached by a raw-boned, wispy-bearded young man, a young man who had barely enough flesh to cover his long bones. In his lanky, rusty-haired, knob-jointed ugliness, he had seemed less intimidating than the more smooth-faced, opaque-mannered young men she met in her classes or at church. She had not been afraid of him, and so she had talked to him, listened when he explained about his work on sea birds, and had him all to herself the whole evening.

To be sure, she did not always understand what he was talking about. White bears, he said. A society of white bears, who exchange secret vows with smoke. You can see the gouges in the walls of houses. Their warnings. You can see their neon tags on the boles of the cedars. They want to put their own gloss on the scripts in my head. He said this patiently, but as if she should be able to figure it out on her own, too.

It was poetry, she thought, like Ecclesiastes or The Revelations of St. John the Divine on the Isle of Patmos. She waited for his pause. Would she be expected to provide an extemporaneous close reading? That did not seem fair. She stood on one foot, then the other, remembered not to bite a hangnail.

She asked, What do they say about your dreams, the animals? She thought that she was being intelligent, to ask this. But his eyes, which had been meeting hers in an open gaze, now narrowed and hardened.

I can't keep doing the work for you. You'll have to figure it out yourself.

She blushed. Okay, she said.

He was twenty-seven, a Ph.D. student.

Then they had made arrangements to go see something in his lab, and for a hike, and another hike, and she saw that she was spending all of her free time with him. He called her a lot. She did not have any close personal friends with whom to discuss him; she fell into his life activities, his energy, as into a vortex.

He lived alone, austerely, with a mattress on the floor and camping equipment and stacks of animal skulls piled against the walls. They lay side-by-side reading their textbooks during the long rainy days and still she did not think of him as a boyfriend. Then one day he put his large-knuckled paw on the small of her back and kissed her nape, and when she turned her face toward him in surprise, her mouth.

Then he began to kiss her more, and to undo her clothing, and she said, I am a virgin. She meant this as an apology for her lack of experience, which was soon to be revealed, but the young man said, I respect that, and even if I never do more than kiss the tips of your fingers, I will devote my whole life to you.

This was, surprisingly, a disappointment to her. When she encouraged him to continue to move his ginger-furred hands under her clothing, he said, We should get married. There were so many good excuses for not inviting family and friends – distance, penury, scheduling – that she was not even remotely troubled by the possibility of other motives for their secrecy and haste.

It was final exam time. For their honeymoon, they would spend a month on a remote West Coast island, where he would be doing his research. There would not be electricity or internet on the island – they wouldn't even have a phone. That made her feel safe from something.

HE IS HER HUSBAND. He is twenty-seven. He is studying gannets, a kind of white seabird with black lines around its eyes and bill, like the lead in stained glass windows. He has a beard, wears real boots with steel toes and laces, plaid flannel shirts. She has never met anyone who knows as much as he does. They have been married for three weeks.

In their tent under the giant dark trees and the many distant stars, he tells her about the animals on the island: their habitats, their behaviours, their secret communications.

She is not sure about the white bears. That's another island, further south, isn't it? The white bears, the spirit bears. She has read about them in *National Geographic*.

What kinds of animals?

In the three weeks they have been on the island, she has seen these: a white-footed mouse, running across the tent platform; two raccoons, washing stolen beef jerky in the stream; four Steller's jays, trying to rip open a package of instant noodles, stolen from the table; some small birds that may have been finches, calling *zonk, zonk* in spruce; a woodpecker; a bald eagle; a flotilla of surf scoters bobbing offshore, in the open waves.

She has not seen any bears, nor a cougar, though the skipper who dropped them at the beach had warned them.

She has not seen the gannets. The gannets nest on the cliffs. He doesn't want her to tag along when he is working. She will corrupt the observation site, simply by her presence. She has to stay at the camp.

He goes to the cliffs five times in two weeks: the first three times in the first week.

It rains every day. Even when it is not raining, the cedars drip. Everything they own is damp. They spend a lot of time trying to dry out their clothes and their sleeping bags.

When he has gone to the cliffs she reads, but she has read everything she has brought, now, all of the novels. She is reading his field guides and notes, and then makes tiny forays into the trees and underbrush around their camp to identify vegetation, and, if she's lucky, animals. She ventures only as far as she can without losing sight of the orange fly of their tent.

The wet cedars and the underbrush smell like cat pee. She thinks it is the cougar, but he says no, underbrush just smells like that. She doesn't complain because he is working, but the days he goes to the cliffs are as long as weeks, and at the end of them she is hollowed out, empty as the crab claws on the shingle beach. She then has no thoughts, no sense of herself thinking. She's scoured out like a rock pool. Only panic running in her head, a small engine. She tries to remember the pattern in the living room carpet, at home, questions on exams, her grandmother's voice, but it's all gone. All she has is the noises of the underbrush, the endless dripping. When he returns on those days she has no words left: she has petrified, toes to ears. Only then with his talk, he brings her back to life, inch by inch.

A great deal of their time is taken up with cooking and eating. In the first week, bacon and eggs, but now canned food: salmon and tuna and corned beef, mini-ravioli and stew or beans. Protein. Twice, mussels chiseled off the rock face at low tide, tasting of salt, of blood, of herself on his beard. He forages for chanterelles and morels and fiddleheads, though he won't show her where to find them. Cougar, he says. And once he brought back a big blue crab, not really enough meat for both of them, but they'd made pancakes, after, eaten them with a jar of jam. He had stabbed the crab in the water, wading barefoot, his toes, he said, completely numb. It was June, a month without an R, but still safe for seafood he said, because of the cold currents hugging the island. No red tide algae. She was surprised and somehow disturbed to find a scientific basis behind what she thought was folklore. What other prohibitions, recently shucked off, would she find out had a legitimate basis? She felt the ground was crumbling under her.

When she's alone for the day she eats crackers and peanut butter.

She thinks that the cliffs are the source of the good days, of his energy. On the days he does not go to the cliffs, in the third week, she thinks about saying, why don't you go to the cliffs, it always seems to cheer you up. But she does not say this, because he had told her at the beginning that she could never tell him what to do, give him advice. This was on the first day, when they were putting up the tent, and she'd said, What about here, here's good, and he had said, Don't ever do that. I'm the boss here, okay? I am used to wilderness living. You're not. It could be life and death, and I won't have time to explain it or argue with you every time.

Okay, she had said. Her chin had trembled.

After he has stopped going to the cliffs, he spends hours lying silently in their zipped-together sleeping bags, and won't eat or talk to her, turns his face away as if she's done something wrong, or paces around their campsite as if it is enclosed by an invisible fence. In those hours she doesn't know what to do; she has run out of reading material. She decides she will reread some of her novels, but if she tries to read he shuts her book, silently, reproachfully.

He doesn't like her to read fiction: he says that she likes fiction because her brain is still adolescent, immature. She should wake up to the real world. She thinks this is at least partly true. She doesn't know what these stories really have to do with her life, though she is good at composing neat, well-constructed essays about them.

She reads over and over the folklore anthology she has brought along, which he doesn't object to. Her mind, which reads and sees the patterns in realistic stories so adroitly, can't make head nor tail of these fables and *contes*. It's as if her brain can't even pay attention properly to the words. She has to piece them out bit by bit, as if she's learning to read all over again. But she feels them seep into the cells of her body.

THEN THE RAIN STOPS and the sun comes out and she puts her head into the tent and says, Rise and shine, sleepyhead! Going to the nests today? But he groans, pulls his pillow over his face. For the first time, she feels a puff of impatience towards him. That's rude, she thinks, and immature. Come on, she says, pulling at the pillow. You haven't been out on the cliffs for a week. You need to do your research.

He pulls the pillow more tightly then and makes a sound she has never heard him – or another adult – make before, a sound somewhere between a whimper and a snarl.

Suit yourself, she says.

She makes herself a pot of porridge and eats it. Then she drags her duffel bag with all of her clothes out of the tent and hangs her damp jeans and t-shirts and jackets up on the clotheslines – everything except what she has on. She washes her underwear and socks and hangs them too.

Now their campsite looks like a medieval fair, the metal of poles shining in the sun, the orange tent, the flapping of her clothes like gay banners. It's very cheerful. It lifts her spirits. It's like the king is going to appear, on a white horse.

She carries water from the stream, fills all of their containers, putting in the potassium permanganate crystals. She decides she'll go for firewood, save him the work, and takes the tarp bag and the axe and sets off into the sparkling forest.

When she has gathered as much as she can carry, she begins her journey back to the campsite. But even before she's through the trees she can smell it, the smoke that isn't wood smoke. She doesn't let go of the tarp bag she's dragging, but begins to walk faster, so that it bangs into roots and trees along the deer path. Then, at the edge of the clearing, she lets go and runs.

All of her clothes have been taken down from the clotheslines and are smouldering on their campfire.

Ohmygodohmygodohmygod, she says. Her husband is sitting, dressed, on a campstool, whittling. When he looks up at her, he's calm: There's a glint of humour in his eyes.

Time to see what you're made of, girl, he says, affectionately.

Is it a metaphor for something?

She hears a voice – her grandma's or a prof's – saying, *think*, and she does try to think. She tries to reason her way into a clear understanding of her dilemma and a way out of it, but the problem is that the problem is *him*, and whatever she thinks, he is there ahead of her. Even though he has put all of her clothes on the campfire, which was not a sane thing to do, and even though (she realizes it now) at least from their second week on the island, but maybe before that, maybe even since they met, he has been saying and doing things that are not exactly *sane*, he can still think faster than she can.

I suppose you're saying to yourself that I've lost it, he says. But what evidence do you really have? You're just applying your preconceived notions of social propriety.

I suppose you're thinking about leaving me here alone, he says, but you know the boat isn't coming back for two more weeks. You're not going to hide in the woods – cougar, remember? I don't think you're strong enough to hurt me while I'm sleeping. I haven't hurt *you*, anyway.

You're right, he says. It makes sense that I've got a way of contacting the mainland in an emergency, but if I haven't told you where or what it is already, I'm not likely to now, am I?

I'm disappointed in your lack of trust, and loyalty, he says. I thought you were exceptional, that you were wiser and braver and more unselfish than the others. But I see that you're not.

She can't think fast enough. She can't think of what to do or say. Every argument, every plea she makes, he blocks. She can't find a way around him. She can't think her way out.

In her fear, then, she gives in to instinct. She does the one thing that seems possible. She takes off all of the clean clothes she is wearing, her shorts and sweatshirt, her panties and bra, and she folds them up and puts them on his lap, and looks steadily into his eyes.

That's better, he says. He doesn't put her clothes on the fire; he places them, ceremoniously, on the camp stool beside him.

She's soon cold: It's always cold, on the island. She feels too naked; she feels she has been skinned. But when she reaches for her clothes, he puts his arm out, a barrier, shakes his head, says, "Unh-unh-unh."

So she takes his hand, pulls him up, begins to undo his clothes. She takes off his flannel shirt and his shorts, the flip-flops he wears in their camp, his underwear. She leads him to the stream, and they squat in the stream together, and she cups her hands to bring water to his forehead and his mouth, and talks to him soothingly, playfully, admiringly, as she would her cat.

BY NIGHTFALL she's sunburned and covered with mosquito bites, and has not eaten since the porridge. She says, for the fifth time, May I cook? I'm so hungry. May I get dressed? I'm so cold.

And he says, finally, Yes, cook. Yes, put your clothes on. He daubs mud on her bites, and she on his, and he puts on his clothes, too: long pants and a sweatshirt.

She makes the fire come back, and stirs a couple of packages of pasta mix into a pot of water, the quickest thing she can think of. She's so hungry!

After they've eaten, he crawls into the tent and falls asleep, and she stays by the fire and tries to think.

While he's sleeping, she crawls into the tent and starts to go through his duffel bag, but he wakes up and grabs her wrist hard, and twists it, and snarls at her. Then he won't go back to sleep, but sits by the fire, his head jerking every now and then, keeping himself awake. He has the duffel bag between his feet.

She means to stay awake all night, watching him, but she can't: She falls asleep by the fire in her sleeping bag, which she has unzipped from his. In the morning she sees that he has kept the fire going. He brings her water, makes porridge. She thinks she won't eat or drink, and then she does: There doesn't seem any point in refusing.

In the morning he goes to the cliffs. As soon as he is gone, she dives at his bag, but of course the radio is not there. In the afternoon he comes back from the cliffs whistling so she will know it is him rustling through the salmonberry and salal and not the cougar. Comes back whistling, strips off his backpack and his binoculars and his Gore-Tex, his flannel shirt, his gabardine work pants, which are all coated with white and black smears, gannet guano. Builds up the fire, which she hasn't tended properly, which has burned down to sullen coals. Balances the big black kettle on the flat stones, boils the water for washing himself and his clothes. Hangs his clothes not on the line but over the boughs of the cedars, which only he can reach. Nude and whistling in the clearing.

In the tent that night, he says, We're part of a larger experiment. We could have everything. Don't ruin it. She recalls now his stories of previous girlfriends, their perfidy, their inexplicable betrayals and sudden abandonments. She hears her grandmother saying, You made your bed; now you have to lie on it.

He doesn't go to the cliffs that day, but crouches by the fire. He says he's thinking; he doesn't want to be disturbed. Later, he talks again about the cougar that menaces their camp. He says, If you could see its trails at dawn, they'd glow, like tail lights in time-lapse photographs. He says, If you could read its dark ammoniac trails, you could see that the cougar is stalking our dreams. He says he wishes they had a fence, but he will protect her. And she says she knows he will.

Is there even a cougar?

She wakes to find that he has tied the bear bells to the outside of the tent zipper. She sees that he is going to catch naps while she's asleep, and remain alert when she's awake. She teaches herself to hold perfectly still in the tent when she is awake, and to sleep for a few minutes only: to swim to the bottom of sleep, just till dreams begin, and come right back up for air.

She wakes to find that he has smashed their remaining cans of food with rocks, has opened all of the packets and plastic bags and Tupperware and poured all of their contents on the ground, ground them into the thin coniferous-forest soil.

How many days before they will be picked up? She can't remember. She gets back into her sleeping bag, closes her eyes. The smell of her unwashed body and clothes is somehow comforting. She hugs her knees to her chest. She is sinking back into the ground, a pod, a pupa, something furred and curled on itself, earthing itself for the winter.

But then at dawn she crawls out of the tent to go into the woods and pee, and though the bear bells jingle, she sees that he is asleep on the ground outside the tent, and even when she calls his name and prods him with a stick, he doesn't wake up.

She knows what to do, now. Her brain tells her in a series of clear images.

THE HELICOPTER ARRIVES AT DAWN, on a Wednesday. She does not know that it is a Wednesday. She has kept the fire going, even though she could only find wet wood, and the helicopter comes straight from the sea to the clearing and sets down, the wind from the propellers blowing the fire out and battering the tent, making it fling itself sideways and strain against its pegs and cords as if it contained a wild beast.

Even when the helicopter blades have stopped spinning she does not rise from where she has been crouching, by the fire, almost in the ashes; where she has been holding the radio against her for several hours, pressed against her chest. Two people get out of the helicopter: the pilot and her husband's supervisor. She points and stays in her crouch while they open the tent, while they enter the tent where she has put him to keep him out of the rain. She waits for them to see him as she has left him, as she has had to leave him, in his fouled cocoon of duct tape and sleeping bag and more duct tape. She waits for their cries of reproach, of anger at her cruelty. She braces herself so that she will not shake. She has not eaten for three days, and she is soaked with rain, and it is hard not to shake.

He has said he will tell them it was all her: her madness, her burning of the clothes, her grinding of the food supplies into the ground. He has said that they will believe him. Her hair is snarled and there is dirt on her face. She doesn't know if they will believe him.

But she does not care much. There will be blankets and hot food, soon, but even that does not matter much. Something new and foreign, but at the same time, utterly hers, has taken possession of her, has entered her bloodstream, permeated the membranes of her cells. She tenses and relaxes her joints, secretly: her shoulders, her knees, her jaws. She feels their quick vital response. She feels the pure clear force in her own sinews. She feels her nails growing, her teeth shining white inside her head. She sees in a kind of vision of herself, the inside of her own body: that she is made of sinew and thick red muscle and living, glistening bone.

She feels a sudden fierce joy pulse through her. What is it?

They are coming out of the tent, now, the two men. They are half-carrying, half-dragging something. She stands up to meet them. She is not afraid.

THAT
ERSATZ
THING

IN ITS PRESENT INCARNATION the restaurant is pretending to be Cuban, and framed black-and-white photographs of Fidel Castro and Che Guevara line the long galley walls: They look somehow as if they've been torn from old copies of *Life* magazine. There are cigar-ad posters, too. One reads, with odd formality, *Accept No Substitutes*. Mirrors with ornate gilded frames. Underneath, the walls have been painted a deep oxblood, and below that is a layer of tarnished gold. Below that, white. You can see all the layers where the walls have been scarred by scratched initials and graffiti, all the way along the wooden booths. I wonder about the graffiti: Was it there before? I don't remember it. It occurs to me that the paint might have been scratched intentionally, for effect. Faded grandeur, that's the phrase.

The menu seems similar to what it was last time we were here, ten years ago, except that there was fruit in everything. I remember Patrick deconstructing the selections. Ordering the spiced-peach blackened chicken salad, and telling the server to hold the peaches.

"But it's a *peach* salad," she had said. "You want peach salad, but no peaches?"

"That's right," Patrick had said, smiling at the server with exactly the same degree of attention, the same warmth of smile (all white teeth and crinkly eyes) that he offers me.

The fruit has gone from the menu. It must have been a fad. Now it's seafood, beans, guacamole. Pulled and jerked meat. Will it be too ordinary for Patrick? But he's smiling over the menu.

Seeing Patrick after a hiatus, I'm always dazed, like when you walk from a dim room into sunlight. There's somehow too much of him, too much intensity. I look forward so much to seeing him, and then I have to look away. I have conversations with him in my head for months or years, and then I am unable to speak.

I wait to see what Patrick will order, before I decide. There's an art to ordering sympathetically. You have to order something complementary: not the same, but not in an entirely different universe. When there's a big menu, I want to have a kind of tree diagram in my mind. If a, then b.

He says, "There's so much. So much meat."

"Beans, then," I say.

"But I haven't had a lot of meat lately."

He will decide on the mussels or the pulled pork taco.

"Do you think the mussels?" he asks, irradiating me with his crinkled eyes, his teeth.

Patrick looks back at the menu, the laminated trifold leaflet, and I finally look at him properly. Seeing Patrick after a hiatus, I think, there are always a few seconds when his face seems altered, strange. In those few seconds, I can feel detached, separate. It's just a face. But then there's that moment of intense recognition, of realization that all the faces I've seen in the interim have been inferior copies of this ideal model. Then I do not know if I could describe him objectively, if I were asked.

The server comes, and Patrick orders the pulled pork, and I'll have the coconut chicken, and the server flirts with Patrick and asks for his autograph, and I wait, and Patrick asks if I'll have sangria, and I say yes and smile, and wait. The gallery is lit by a row of large-bladed ceiling fans, each with a light fixture in the shape of a cluster of fluted glass bells. The fans are the kind of thing you associate with the Habitat for Humanity warehouse, or your grandparents' dining room in the cheaper suburbs. Here, though, they seem glamorous, authentic. They say *Plantation*, not *Abbotsford*. It occurs to me that in their original context, the fans with their glass bells are meant to mimic a tropical flower, and that they are not kitschy at all, but romantic, sensual. I suddenly see that the faux-wood of the blades is meant to be bamboo, and that the flowers would be deep-coloured, thickly-scented blooms that would hang heavy and lush and cool on night patios. The fans would stir the warm, dense, tropical air. In a room in which tendrils crept over the windowsills during the night, in which heavily-scented air lapped slowly, like a drawn bath, around you, the little glass bells would not be ersatz, but organic.

Under the warm lights the server is flushed, a rising of blood in her downy transparent skin. I see the name on her tag is Saffron. She's young enough for it to be her real name.

I feel flushed too, the heat in my face and neck, along my collarbones.

I wait for Patrick and the server to conclude their transaction, and two things occur to me. The first is that I am too tired to go through this again – the disappearance and reappearance, the sudden excitement, the disappointment, the internal rages of jealousy, the clamping down on my own yearning.

The second thing that occurs to me is that I must find a new way of *being*, with Patrick, now that we apparently are going to pick up our relationship again. I have no more energy for irony, for self-abasement. I see that I have a choice, that I can either disappear, cease to be part of Patrick's set décor, or find a new way, which is true and yet will not destroy the delicate equilibrium.

"I like this place," Patrick says, when the server has taken her too-aware self off. He always says that. He never remembers that he's been here before.

"So, you're back in town," I say, and feel my shoulders hunch. That was lame.

Twenty years ago, Patrick and I sat in a chilly wind on the sea wall in False Creek. He was downcast, having broken up with yet another beautiful, insanely self-absorbed actor, and I, as usual, was applying first aid. And then I made my big mistake. I knew it was a mistake, that by speaking I would lose the pleasures of our friendship, that what I was about to do would be seen only as a declaration of war, but I was driven by a kind of despair, a desperation to have something of Patrick beyond the plays that I helped him build.

"There's always me, Patrick," I said.

His answer was so quick and appropriate that it sounded rehearsed. "That's very flattering, Chris," he said. "But you know, I just can't see my way to it." He behaved so beautifully that I can't even remember which of us stopped calling first.

So, you see, I've learned my lesson. But how can I talk to Patrick, if I am to abandon my facetious, flippant ways, and yet not admit, in every sentence, my futile love?

There's a channel-changing pause, and then Patrick says, "My series bombed."

"I know," I respond. I admitted a long time ago to my possibly obsessive collecting of Patrick's press clippings. Patrick gives his trademark self-deprecating grimace: corners of the mouth pulled down, eyes widened. It's harder than it looks. When I try that expression, it turns out like a sad clown's.

"American TV," I say. "All people want is mindless entertainment."

It's a conversation we've had before. I'm good at this role, laying down my cloak. I'm good at this, being one of the invisible people who hold up the expressive and the famous. Good at being a channel, humble, effaced.

But Patrick frowns, a real frown, creases marring his perfect forehead, his upper lip pulling back and thinning. I notice now that his skin has thickened, that the flesh of his cheeks has migrated, almost imperceptibly, from his cheekbones towards his jaw.

"Did you see it?" he asks.

I did. I watched the series, only because Patrick was in it. He'd played a blue-collar single-dad cop, one who bucked the rules, messed up, skated close to trouble, but always went with his gut, and was validated in the end. The real criminal caught; the line in the sand re-drawn. I had thought it glib, clichéd, full of holes, both logical and thematic.

After the series ended, Patrick had gone to England for a stage role, filling in as a police detective in what Wikipedia calls "a long-running West End farce." I hadn't seen it, of course.

I ask about the stage play now, though I know from Patrick's website that it has folded, but he uses it as a segue into a different subject.

"After things didn't work out in London, I had a few weeks before my next job. I made a trip to my grandfather's birthplace."

And now I prick up my ears. I already know a little bit about Patrick's trip, from Allan, who's one of my clients, and I remember that Patrick's grandparents came from there – the very old walled city, in a country of old rifts and passions that has, in the last year, flared into violence. So it was a pilgrimage. I can see Patrick being into that.

"Did you find the house?"

"I did," Patrick says.

There is another pause; Patrick gazes at his plate. "It is a fabulous city," he says. "It's over a thousand years old, you know. There are stone streets and buildings, still, packed in with modern concrete and glass, and bombed-out brick, from the last war. And it's much denser than cities here; there's much more sense of life."

I've seen the city, on television, quite a lot over the last few months. I can see it now, the river with its stone bridges running like a dark vein through it, the clamorous mixture of old and new streets, Patrick winding his way through them, led by a salmonid instinct.

"And?"

Patrick shrugs. "It was an interesting place to see, that's all. Very photographic. Atmospheric."

The story is there, but out of reach: a dark shape under river ice. But I am not able to retrieve it. And Patrick changes the subject, again, and tells me about his new deal for a TV show. It should be a hit, I say. But I'm not sure if I'm required to respond, even. The new series is based on one of his early plays, one that I read drafts of, years ago. It was about an Italian-immigrant family in the 70s, set in Trail, a mining town in the BC Interior. Lots of jokes about food and church and hockey dads. And the grandmother dies. I remember it. For the TV series, the setting has been moved to a small town in Nevada, but the series is being filmed in Vancouver and Hope.

Patrick is very animated: his eyebrows leap, he laughs a lot, and tells me anecdotes about producers and television actors he's been working with. Only I would notice, perhaps, that he isn't really talking about the series, but giving a kind of performance, as for talk show appearance, and that as he talks, he seems to shift too much, as if his clothing is uncomfortable. What has happened to him, I wonder. He was always the one with the focus, the depth.

"That's great, Patrick," I say, when he comes to a pause.

"Yes," he says. "I am lucky to have this chance."

"So, acting and directing in real television series that you wrote," I say. "Your dreams coming true."

"Yes," Patrick says. But his answer is a dead-end street.

Is it only that we have not talked so long in years that the conversation seems to be taking place on opposite sides of a wall? We do not talk about me, but that's okay; my life isn't very interesting, compared to Patrick's.

OUR MUTUAL ACQUAINTANCE, prone on my 1930s massage table, asks if I have seen Patrick yet. I admit that I have, though I can see that he wants to gossip. He tells me that he, also, has had lunch with Patrick, that Patrick told him all about his trip and his new series.

This client is a nuisance, a sycophant, a gossip. But also a messenger, and necessary.

"I think the series is going to be fabulous," he burbles. "And the important people Patrick's meeting now! Well! He's moved way out of our orbit, hasn't he! But he deserves it. He's so gifted. Some people are just born with it, aren't they? And the rest of us might as well not even try."

"Do you think so?" I murmur, pressing the unsolid flesh at his waist.

"Oh, well, you or I could never accomplish anything like what Patrick does, could we?"

Speak for yourself. But I haven't said this aloud, I realize, after a few apprehensive seconds. The flabby white shoulders, the dimpled posterior, face me with equanimity, the tongue clatters on. How would it be if I were just now to apply too much pressure to the carotids? Would my elderly receptionist help me to dress this client's inert body in his clothes and drag him to a dumpster?

I am worried about myself. Envy: one of the seven deadly sins. At the least, bad karma. But stalking home along my east-side street at dusk, I wonder: Is it that I want Patrick to myself, or want to be him?

At one time I wanted to shine, like Patrick and the others. Instead, I do massage. Ironically, I'm much sought after by the city's glitterati. I minister to the artists, draw out from the muscles of my clients' bodies with my strong and articulate hands their fears and anxieties, the garbage that blocks their creativity. Pain and grief reside not just in the mind, but in the body, in the tissues. It's all technique, of course; it's a matter of training one's hands to be sensitive to the structures under the skin, to controlling the pressure and direction of the hands' movements. I'm an amanuensis of the muscles and cartilage.

A couple of days later, I bump into Patrick on the street near my offices. I'm flustered again at seeing him unexpectedly, and stand there, my hands in my pockets, grinning at him stupidly through the November drizzle.

"Your new office is right on this block, isn't it?" Patrick asks.

Cool sludge settles in my mind. "Yes," I say flatly. I will not make the offer. Then, because he seems to expect it, I invite him to come up and see my workplace, and he accepts with what seems to be eagerness. There isn't much: first, a waiting room, small and painted a soothing shade of taupe and furnished with a desk, a file cabinet, a couch, a mirror, all arranged according to feng shui principles, and inhabited by my receptionist, who is actually out for lunch right now. I explain about Dorothy: She's pushing seventy, I'd guess, and people are sometimes surprised to see her working. She needs to work, for reasons she darkly referred to as *choices I made when I was younger*. I assume that they were the kinds of choices that resulted in her having neither spousal support nor a pension plan, and I long to ask her if it was worth it. I hired her because I could only admire someone who had been so impractical. But she is extraordinarily competent; she understands computers and filing systems in a way that I don't, and manages the clients well, too. They bring her gifts.

Besides the reception area there are two other rooms, one for changing, one for my work, and a lavatory that I share with the accountant next door. I show Patrick my table, which I'm proud of, as it took me months to find. It's from the 1930s, and very beautiful and functional. Patrick stands by it for a few moments, absently rubbing the grain of the black leather with one forefinger. Then all at once he hops up onto the table and rolls onto his stomach. He smiles at me, invitingly.

But I am unable to move. In this space, where I am at deep levels of intimacy and relaxation with my clients, I find I can't stand next to Patrick without feeling dizzy. I lean back against the cabinet doors, my arms folded. After a few moments, he swings himself off the table.

"You've got a great space for yourself here," Patrick says. He checks his watch, glances at his reflection in the small round mirror in the waiting room, smoothing his hair with his hand.

"Lunch date?" I ask.

"No," Patrick says, mumbling, almost embarrassed. "Meeting with some TV people." And he's out the door as Dorothy comes in, shaking her umbrella.

She looks curiously at Patrick's back moving down the corridor. "I didn't know you had a booking," she says. "I could have stayed in."

"Not a client," I say. "An old friend stopping by."

"A lovely man," she says. "You just want to *touch* him."

I wince. "I don't usually agree to give massage to my friends," I say. "I need the separation."

Dorothy, pulling out her keyboard tray, rubbing her hands together to warm them, gives me a look I can only describe as pitying. Sometimes I'm jealous of her. I hear, from my inner room, the rise and fall of voices in the waiting room, and I know that she is offering, out there, her own line of therapy. That my clients are disclosing to her what they do not tell me. Hence the gifts.

I imagine confiding in Dorothy. "It's as if," I say in my imagination, "I was imprinted at birth, and nothing can erase that neurological magnetism." Though when I was born, it occurs to me, Patrick was still a pair of gametes, growing separately in the caves of his parents' bodies.

I will not confide in Dorothy.

IN MY APARTMENT, the top floor of a small east-side house, I move around in the dusk, closing the blinds. In the basement suite, the tenants are having their meal. I can hear the subterranean rumble of their voices, clanking of pots, burst of laughter. I sit down to a plate of lettuce and a wedge of cheese, and my usual evening catechism.

Why aren't you happy now that Patrick is back in your life? What is it that you want from him?

Not crumbs. Not a business relationship.

But what? Do you think he is going to just turn up and leap into bed with you?

No. No. Though I would have gone to bed with him in a minute, even a year ago, it almost seems too late for that now, between Patrick and me. The humidity, the carnality of sex. My desire feels to me now an ancient tree, beautiful in its bleakness.

Do you want domestic intimacy? To make his coffee? Wash his socks?

I look around my small suite, my shabby rugs and furniture, the quirky things I have on the walls. It is a private space, hard-won. I have few visitors. I do not often long for company, after a long day of emptying myself.

Long ago, I used to have a fantasy about Patrick: He'd become ill – something serious and wasting, but not *too* serious, not AIDS or anything like that, and he'd have to stay with me, and I'd take care of him, sponging his body, taking notes while he dictated delirious amendments to his script. In my fantasy, he'd take my hand and look up at me, his eyes feverish, and whisper, "It's a gift, what you do." And

I'd be safe, preserved forever in my usefulness. But I have learned something, in the last few years, about giving and owning.

Recognition? Is that it? You want to go about socially as a couple? Attend Patrick's premieres, have your picture with his in the entertainment section of the newspaper?

I am incapable of even imagining that.

There's a knock on my door then, and I hear after the fact the sound of footsteps ascending the outside staircase to my back door. When I open it, it's Mrs. B, from downstairs, with a steaming, covered bowl.

"I hear again no cooking," she says.

It looks as if she will stand there until I eat, so I get a spoon and sit down, and she sits, watching. It's a good soup, more of a potage, full of barley and rich juices. When she takes the bowl and goes back downstairs, it's as if I have been thawed and brought back to life. Everything aches, but I am weepy with relief.

I FIND MYSELF WAYLAYING Dorothy after the last client one afternoon, as she's putting on her coat and scarf. I want to have him; I want him to love me. I know I cannot own him. But I want, I want. How is it that one can love and not be loved in return? How is it that one can find in another person the precise complement to one's soul, one's missing half, and yet not appear that way to the other? I am unable to get past this, but I must move on. I say all this as though confessing a mortal sin. She must give me comfort, advice. Absolution.

Her pouched old eyes glitter at me. "Oh, shame, shame," she says, mockingly, over her shoulder, as she walks out of the office.

Old sibyl. Old witch.

But for a moment or two after Dorothy leaves, the room shakes, as if it's been hit by an earthquake or a bomb. It's a tremor from the construction going on next door. I reel against a high cabinet; a package leaps from its shelf and I am baptized in a shower of plastic spoons.

I understand now what I have been seeking. I know very well that I've withheld my touch from Patrick out of self-protection, so that I would have something of myself that I had not offered to him. I see now what I require, what is required of me.

My clients sometimes ask me if it is true that the human body isn't designed for walking upright, that we're not quite evolved enough from our ancestors who carried their bodies on four limbs, parallel to the earth, that our spines are subject to intense stress because of our unnatural gait. It's a myth, I tell them. While it is true that most adult humans suffer from pain, and the pain seems to stem from that attenuated question mark, the spine, our spines are, in fact, perfectly engineered for our posture. The balance of our hips and ribcages, the swing of our shoulder bones, the rotating suspension of our hip sockets are all miracles of engineering design. We are as beautifully and ergonomically put together as trees.

The problem is our heads. They are much too heavy, with their solid bony brain cases, their double handful of dense grey material inside. It is the weight of our heads that compresses our disks, that locks our joints, that seizes up our limbs.

I reach for Dorothy's appointment book, and the telephone.

THE DAY THAT I am to see Patrick, I experience almost debilitating stage fright. It's been years since I've touched his body. Will the experience be too poignant? Will I forget what I do?

When I come into the room where I work, he lies prone on my table, wearing only the white towel. I warm my hands with scented oil, greeting him, as I greet all of my clients, with questions: Is the room warm enough? The background music acceptable?

I must start. I begin, as I would begin with any new client, by reading his body with my fingers. He has filled out somewhat, my fingers see, though they recognize the texture of his skin, the map of his tendons and muscles, almost instantly. The last five years are a mere sheen of oil between my hands, his skin.

And when I touch him, Patrick falls into his story with a kind of gracelessness that is grace, like a child falling into water, or leaves, or bed, and I recognize that at last it is himself he is offering.

"When I found my grandfather's house," he says, "I decided to knock on the door."

"Yes, of course," I say.

"And the woman who opened it," he says, "was my second cousin. Imagine it: My family was still living in the same house that my grandfather and great-grandfather were born in."

"Did you recognize her?" I ask.

There's a pause, and then Patrick says, "My own face."

I can see her, in my imagination. The same spade-shaped face, the same full curving lower lip, the brows like smears of machine grease.

"But dark-haired," Patrick says, his voice travelling an unimaginable distance, and in his voice I can see her, leaning in an ancient doorway, her lips curving. I can hear her skewed, seductive English. The romance of history, of the familiar seen awry, the self on another trajectory – she would have had it all. And in that one instant Patrick would have believed that he was seeing the person he had been searching for all his life.

I could tell him something about recognition, about being transfixed by the geometry of a face, a voice. "Did she recognize you?" I ask.

"Not really," Patrick says. "People over there aren't looking for their roots, you know? If a relation turns up from America, they think you're rich, they think you can help them immigrate."

I understand his new, flat, careful intonation, now. I know now why he has sought me out, though I doubt he realizes it yet. We are citizens of the same country, now, or non-country. We're fellow exiles.

I HAD BOOKED PATRICK for the last appointment of the day, and when we finish up, Dorothy has already gone home. Patrick emerges from the changing room just as I'm done with my tidying, and we walk out of the building together. It's dusk; the rush-hour traffic is already thinning, and we walk down the street towards the Skytrain station, towards the Italian and Portuguese shops, the bakeries and tile stores and photo labs. Our arms brush, our strides match. We carry our silence as a comfortable burden.

Spread out below us, to the north and west, the city's lights are springing, reassuringly, to life. At night they form a huge dished web, torn at one edge by a black space where the ocean is, but for now the outlines of buildings and streets can still be made out; the city is still intact. Poised on a fault line, it is; cratered, rigged to trip, fibrillate, detonate. But how it glitters, how it connects and illuminates, an illusory web, but, at night, really all that we have.

VAGINA DENTATA

AFTER THE CONFERENCE, in which we distinguished ourselves modestly on a number of issues – the colonial, the
survival, the post-colonial, the post-survival, the structur-
alist, the deconstructivist, the Freudian, the feminist, the
body, and the post-body – the organizers – that is, those of
us who always do the shit work around here – took the strag-
glers, those who were not sufficiently important enough to
have other conferences to attend the next day in Toronto or
Montreal or Corner Brook, to a lake in the mountains, where
one of the indefatigable and perpetually subjugated organizers had organized the loan of a cottage.

We went in a cortège of vehicles, half of which were grey
Toyota Corollas, two of which were blue Honda Civics, one
of which was a shabby minivan. Some of us who had lived

in the city and taught at the institution for seventeen years had never been to this lake before, which others of us found surprising, as it is a mere half-hour drive from campus, and surprisingly cool and fresh in the summer. Some of us wondered if this lacuna was attributable to mental rigidity and/or disaffection, or whether it was an indication that some of us had more cosmopolitan lives than others, and spent summers at more distant, up-market lakes, or perhaps not at lakes at all – perhaps entombed in the subterranean archives of old British universities, or kayaking with only a giant bottle of mosquito repellant and a waterproof clipboard up inaccessible northern rivers.

Some of us who came up to this lake every year, though, wondered insecurely if we should be spending our summers in more exciting ways – if we had been wasting our meagre summer terms on unimportant, unexciting, and unproductive activities. Some of us wondered if that should be blamed on our spouses.

Some of us marvelled, as the vehicles we were driving or passengering wound higher into the hills, that the slopes surrounding the lake were thickly wooded, lush, velvety, dense with many shades of jade and emerald and perhaps also jadeite and peridot and malachite. Some of us reasoned out that these hills must be the backsides of the sere bluffs that can be seen from the university college campus. Some of us felt that distinct sensation of decompression around the diaphragm which accompanies the realization that one has been, for a substantial length of time, excluded from a desirable experience, compensation, or recognition, such as invitations to the dean's sailing trips or access to the bargain sales of chops by the meat-cutting school on Thursdays.

All of us were impressed to find that the rented cottage was stocked with fishing gear, canoe, kayak, inflatable rowboat, air-mattresses, children's inflatable devices not to be used as life-saving devices, and beach towels, as well as a full complement of cookware and dinnerware and two barbecues. All of us observed the sign on the door that read, in a non-scanning iambic couplet: *If there's sand between your toes/kindly use this hose.* Many of us read it aloud. All of us winced, though some inwardly, at the dropped scansion, which some felt, synesthetically, as a bodily sensation of tripping.

Some of us noted, with disappointment, that there was not actually a beach, but that the lawn ran down a rather steep slope from the cottage to a reed-choked foreshore. Some of us noted that there was a substantial dock, which extended past the reeds, for lounging on and swimming from. Some of us helped carry coolers full of cold drinks and meats, and plastic bags full of buns and condiments and paper plates and napkins into the cottage. Some of us unfolded outdoor chairs and began inflating devices with a foot pump, or our lips. Some of us appropriated the wooden Adirondack chairs immediately, and some accepted lesser chairs of aluminum tubing and polypropylene webbing.

Some of us began to strip down to our bathing suits, and some of us felt trepidation, perhaps even horror, at the prospect of observing and being observed by our colleagues, many of whom had behaved to us in the past, especially in Faculty Council meetings, in ways that did not make us feel emotionally safe in their presence, in a state of undress. Some of us observed silently that the greater power an individual enjoyed in the professional context, the more clothing he or she removed. Some of our female colleagues wore unflattering loose cotton capri trousers and shirts, and large-brimmed hats, and we remembered with discomfort their radiation treatments – was that four or five years ago now? Some of our male colleagues wore black socks with shorts and sandals, and some of us wondered if it might be time for them to retire and relinquish the helm to younger, more energetic faculty with more current research interests.

Some of the younger, more energetic faculty, who were competing for tenure-track positions, had not slept the past week, what with dealing with last-minute cancellations by presenters, "miscommunications" with the caterers, the printers, and the room-booking office, and a grant funds cheque requisition that was buried on an accounts payable clerk's desk. Nevertheless, these faculty, even though their contracts had expired and they weren't being paid, helped make salads and open new bottles of ketchup and mustard, and were cheerful and kind to each other. Most of them wore short denim cut-offs or long cotton sundresses with their swimsuits underneath, or board shorts. But although they looked like twenty-four-year-old Californians, they were, in fact in their mid-thirties already and wondering when they would be able to buy houses and get parental leave benefits.

Only two of the group were children – siblings, and offspring of one of the indefatigable organizers. Children were not generally encouraged at this institution.

SOME OF US WERE SURPRISED to see how plump the plenary speaker was, when she came out of the cottage wearing a shiny black one-piece and an unstructured kimono printed with gingko leaves. Some of us reflected that her publicity photo must be at least fifteen years out of date. Some of us thought of the popular novels she published under a pseudonym, featuring a slim elegant workaholic female detective. Some of us repressed thoughts that her novels were more interesting than her literary criticism. Some of us repressed thoughts that her detective novels, and in fact detective novels in general, are reactionary, or at least passé. Some of us wondered if we could dash out a detective novel in the remaining two months of summer, and thus at some future date, perhaps even as early as the next fall, be able to afford not to teach four sections of introductory composition.

Soon, all of us were on the dock. Most of us looked different, smaller in the outdoors. Some had the sleek, well-developed calves of runners, and a very few had boxer's abs and biceps – who would have imagined it! – while more had the spindle-shanks and hollow chests of older men. On some, the flesh on the ribs drooped, as if losing to gravity, and even the aureole of the nipples was pulled down and to the side and formed the shape of oblongs on the diagonal.

Among those of us who were women, there was more variation in shape and size. Some of us older women wore skirted Full Body Slimming suits that appear to be held up by whalebone – as our grandmothers would have worn – and, spider veins and upper-arm flaps notwithstanding, were nearly covered up sufficiently by our swimsuits to have appeared without embarrassment in front of our classes. One of us, a professor of contemporary Quebec literature, wore a crocheted string bikini and a navel ring. In general we tried to pretend that we did not have bodies, and to contribute to the intellectual tone.

Some of us attempted to continue a discussion that had begun in one of the last sessions of the conference. Some of us taught in this area and had important and useful ideas about it. Most of us had opinions about it.

Some mentioned Sheila Watson and Ethel Wilson, in the context of the geographical setting of this small new university. Some remarked that Canadian Modernism really lagged behind European Modernism by about thirty years. Some of us wondered if there was any point studying it, so late and out of date. One of the indefatigable organizers, whose research and teaching area is Canadian Modernism, blinked her slightly protuberant eyes a couple of times as if the lids are trying to wipe a screen.

Some of us said then that most Canadian writing has not even reached the Modernist period, and remains stuck in the Victorian era. One of us said then that Western Canadian writing seemed all to be about remittance men. One of us said that Canadian writers are all still crofters fighting the Enclosures Act. One of us said that it was all about being afraid of Papa, but obsessed with defying him. Some of us said that Canadian fiction is actually Romantic, making claims for Nature and Beauty and Truth in the face of the industrial machine. Others disputed this. Some said that Canadian fiction is all ghost stories. By whom, for example? others demanded. Lists were made: Atwood, of course. Robertson

Davies. Ondaatje. Kroetsch. Urquhart. Vanderhaeghe. All of recent Canadian literature, one of us said, confuses eccentricity for genius, vandalism for iconoclasm. *Are* there vandals in Canada? some of whom are not Canadian asked. Yes, indeed, other non-Canadians said. They scribble on people's garden sheds with spray cans.

The best Canadian novelists, some said, don't write about Canada. They write about American heroes or life in the Gulag or Malaysian prison camps. All the cult of the individual, others said. Where is the social novel, the experimental novel?

Are there no important Canadian novelists, then? some asked. We will permit you the short story, some said. Munro. Although some might say she is really a Scottish writer. Her stories read Scots. Rubbish, some who were Canadian said. Munro is our Chekov. Munro is their Chekov, the non-Canadians agreed, then. The smell of hamburgers and onions had reached the dock.

Some of us arrived late. Some of us complained about the signage on the road, and some pointed out with more precision that the signage was entirely functional; rather the distances in the email directions didn't correspond with the distances on the odometer. Some of us had used our vehicles' GPS systems. Some of us, who had been organizing the conference and barbecue for many weeks, laughed merrily, perhaps maniacally.

There is some competent nature writing, some said as they stood in line with their paper plates. But too literal or too obviously symbolic. It's trying to be Ibsen or Dostoyevsky or Calvino.

Some of us, bending over grills, blasted by heat and smoke and spitting meats asked querulously if there wasn't anything to eat except dead animal. Some of us pointed out that protein-rich salads had been prepared. Some of us wondered, mostly facetiously, if there were any firearms on this property, and if so, if they were securely locked away. Some of us thought this joke in bad taste.

One of us arrived, last of all, on a motorbike and some of us ignored him as he swung a long lean leg easily over the saddle and doffed his helmet and shook out his long hair, which had hardly any grey in it at all. Some of us ignored him as he stepped onto the lawn in his jeans, looking neither spindle-shanked nor pot-bellied. Some of us ignored him as he opened a beer and took over one of the barbecues. Some of us felt, at this point, that the party was only now complete, but didn't understand why we felt this way.

AFTER THE FOOD HAD BEEN CONSUMED, some of us who were the younger faculty – obedient, compliant, untenured – cleaned up, pushing the paper plates and foam cups into oversized black garbage bags, and then sat quietly on the dock, at the admonishment of the older ones, who had had drummed into them at some point, it seems, the warning against swimming after eating. But some of us threw caution to the wind and paddled around knee-deep, or set sail on a flotilla of inflatable ducks and porpoises.

The plenary speaker appropriated the largest air mattress, a huge inflatable chaise with pockets for beverages, and drifted out into the lake with a rather down-market women's magazine and a wide-brimmed straw hat. Some of the Europeans appeared in Speedos. The suits outlined their buttocks, their testicles, their penises. Some of us wondered if we felt intimidated, aroused, or grossed-out. Some of us weren't swimmers; at least, we had lessons at the pool as children, but wouldn't have dreamed of entering this lake, with its mess of reeds and frog spawn and, no doubt, leeches. But some of us dove off the dock and swam out after the plenary speaker, resting our hands briefly on her inflatable throne, then turning and swimming easily back.

One of us, as he hauled himself, dripping, laughing, onto the warm silvered wood of the dock, said: I was afraid out there.

Afraid of what? the rest of us asked.

Of something in the lake, the swimmer said. Something that would eat me.

Vagina dentata, one of the other swimmers suggested.

Yes, I think so, the first swimmer said, squeezing water from his beard.

Some of us didn't know what this meant and had to have it explained. Some of us were discomfited, for differing reasons.

Those of us who were visiting Europeans said: We were just discussing how exciting your life is, and how to express properly our fascination with it. How, if you will forgive us, you live here, with your vast spaces, your new university, at the very edge of terra incognita. How very romantic and glamorous it seems to us!

Those of us who taught at the host institution laughed at the word *glamorous*. Mostly, we said, we felt we were in a backwater, out of the mainstream. Mostly, we said, we felt we had missed the boat.

Oh, no, not missed the boat; flung yourselves from it! those of us who were European visitors answered. Flung yourself in, where you are now swimming among the teeth of the great Mother herself! Some of us wondered at this point how much beer had been consumed and if there would be sufficient sober drivers for the trip back to the city.

Now more of us scrambled into the inflatable dinghies and pushed out into the water, even while arguing over the possession and proper application of the ineffectual plastic oars. Some of us had lost our hats and sunglasses, but the sun had nearly set, anyway. One of us watched the backs of his estranged wife's calves, and then her thighs, mottled with heat rash, disappear into the gelatinous water.

Those of us who had remained on the dock heard a shriek, which one of us recognized as the estranged wife's. Those of us still on the dock rose to our feet. The one who had recognized his wife's scream thought: *my children*. Some of us who were already in the lake already began to swim out to where her head bobbed. One of us, who had just emerged from the lake and was clambering up the somewhat slimy ladder, streaming water, turned and dove back in and was soon past the rest. Some of us thought, admiringly, that she could be mistaken for an Olympic swimmer.

Some of us on the dock didn't know quite what to do. Some of us were still fully dressed. The one of us who had recognized his wife's scream removed his sandals, then wondered aloud: If there is an emergency requiring a car trip, wouldn't it be better to leave them on? He mentioned that he was not a strong swimmer, and that by the time he made it to his screaming wife, he'd be a liability. And there would already be a group of swimmers there.

I felt it, I really did feel it, the one who had screamed kept saying, through chattering teeth. Some of us had been diving among the reeds for nearly an hour, and it was getting dark.

Two of us kept hugging and massaging the one who had screamed. Some of us thought she was enjoying the attention. One of us very gently lifted a corkscrew of damp hair from the cheek of the one who screamed and tucked it behind her ear, in a gesture as intimate as a kiss. *I felt it; I felt it*, the one of us who had screamed said again, and shuddered.

What she had felt, she said, was two things: first, a hand on her thigh, as she was floating along in the water.

Firm or flaccid? one of us interrupted.

One of us wondered if, technically, a hand could be flaccid.

Then, the one who had screamed said, I kicked out violently –

As anyone would, one of us said.

And my feet then connected with a body.

Hard or flaccid, the one of us who had arrived on a motorcycle asked. Some of us detected some irony and tensed.

Oh, soft, the one who had screamed said. I felt the naked skin, the texture. Then the thing drifted away.

No resistance, one of us observed. Dead.

But who is missing? a few of us murmured. It was difficult to determine. Some of us looked around. Some of us had already left. The leaving had been somewhat piecemeal.

Two of us who were sessional faculty had taken the two who were children (but not their own children) with them.

One of us said that it could have been a dog or a deer. After a while in water, the fur comes off – the hide softens.

How do you know this? some of us wondered. But it seemed suddenly to most of us the most likely and satisfactory answer. What the one who screamed had touched in the water was the body of a dog, a deer – perhaps even a bear cub – that had tired while swimming across the lake, or even, months before, had broken through the ice.

Most of us decided, though the decision was not unanimous, to phone the police but not to make it an emergency call. Those of us who hadn't already left disbanded then, loading our bags and damp towels into our Civics and grey Corollas, and drove away. Some of us, who had worked indefatigably to organize the conference and the outing, stayed behind till the last, loading bags of trash and greasy salad bowls into the back of the shabby minivan.

The one who was the plenary speaker also stayed: She had somehow arranged that she would ride back into town on the back of the motorbike. And then the one of us who rode his motorbike to the lake, and the one who would be his passenger left, too, with a clackity roar. That engine was missing something, some of us thought, but we knew nothing about motorcycle engines.

Those of us who were left watched as they turned up the road, the one who was the plenary speaker pressed up against the motorcyclist's back.

Before the two of us who were left, the lake spread, ominous in the dusk. The lake's breeze was suddenly chill. We shivered.

But the air was alive with the sounds of crickets and frogs; their clicks and thrums formed a multi-layered, endless symphonic concert. One of us opened her arms to the vibrating air like a conductor. Both of us heard, then, all of the instruments – the clear optimism of the flute, the self-doubting reeds, the deep froggish complaint of the trombone, and for a few moments, we felt ourselves fully immersed.

THE BISMARCK LITTLE PEOPLE'S ORCHESTRA

MOTHER WAS AGAINST IT, of course. *Vaudeville*, she said, wrinkling up her nose. And: *Remember, Pearl – you are the companions you choose.*

My father was dead, or he'd have raised objections, too. If he's been alive, I wouldn't have got away with it. But I wouldn't have needed to. Father had made a decent living as an accountant. But there was no social safety net back then, for the family of a man killed crossing the street by a drunken milk-truck driver. Mother and I had to scrimp. We were scrimping, and getting scrimpier – shrimpier, too, if that were possible. So when the offer came – my name had been submitted by my music teacher – I jumped on it. I was twenty-one.

Mother got over it. She was practical at heart, even if she did have her little prejudices. I think she even got some mileage out of telling people – not everyone, just people whose sense of propriety she liked to rattle – that I had run away with the circus.

Of course it wasn't the circus. It wasn't even vaudeville. It was a travelling review. You don't know what that is. In my day, in the 30s, reviews were live variety shows that travelled from city to city. The TV variety shows of the 1950s, 1960s – they came out of those reviews.

There were so many travelling reviews that you had to have a gimmick. Sets of triplets or Eskimo throat singers or live elephants. But our whole company was the gimmick.

You've heard that some reviews were off-colour. That is true. There were some pretty sexed-up productions. But our review was completely wholesome.

Well.

Sometimes I wonder about that. Sometimes I wonder if we were a kind of sideshow.

The Bismarck Little People's Orchestra, that's what we were called. We weren't just musicians, though. We all had to dance and sing, as well. So it wasn't just a gimmick. We gave the same entertainment for your dollar – or nickel – as any travelling review.

Me, I played the trumpet. Maybe that's how I got hired. I wasn't quite as little as they liked. Four foot eight. My father played trumpet, and I taught myself, being musical. The orchestra needed trumpet players. They had lots of saxophones – everyone wanted to play the sax. And lots of flautists, though you know, the flute isn't an easy instrument for a little person. It takes as much breath to play a flute as to play a

French horn – most of the air is wasted, blows over the top. But I played the trumpet, and they had only one other trumpeter, who was male.

I'm guessing that's how Jarvis Noakes got hired, too. He was little enough, but his head was a bit large, and his spine was crooked. They didn't want us misshapen or squat or large-headed. We had to be perfectly proportioned. But you don't get many little tuba players.

Now why am I talking about Jarvis Noakes? You'd think I'd start by mentioning Don, who was my boyfriend, my fiancé, I guess. Or Betty, who was my best friend, who I still keep in touch with. Jarvis Noakes! Now there was a sad story. He killed himself. Committed suicide. Many little people do, especially the men. But I don't think he did it for the usual reasons. What are the usual reasons? Well, not being able to cut it in a man's world, I guess. It's easier for small women. Women are supposed to be small. And cute. You know. But for the men – well, I suppose being small is like being defective, for men.

But Jarvis Noakes – no; he did okay in that way. He won the lottery, bought himself a custom-built house, out in California. I saw it, you know. It was a mansion! He won the lottery and retired from the orchestra and it didn't last long after that. We couldn't find another little person to fill his shoes. Ha! But some of us did go see him, in California, when we were touring there.

What was the show like? Well. It was elegant as all get out. We played in formal dress, white tie and tails for the men, long gowns for the girls. Those gowns! They were all different, but we had to be appropriate to the season. We had them custom-designed and made for us, of course. People used to ask me if I could wear little girls' clothes. Of course I couldn't. Little girls don't have hips and bosoms. Mind you, I didn't have much in those days. But I wasn't straight up and down.

I had a red satin gown. Sleeveless, plunging neckline. I believe that got me into trouble, that dress. And three or four green gowns, on account of my hair. You can't tell now, but I was auburn. I had a slinky number, moss-green crepe, cut on the bias. I was particularly fond of that dress. The other girls said it brought out my eyes. Funny, how girls notice things like that and dress for each other. The men liked the red dress. Got their attention, I guess.

And sailor outfits, ethnic outfits. We changed several times a show.

My favourite number? It was a musical theatre piece. "Puttin' on the Ritz." We were all in silver. The audience was always swept away. I guess there wasn't a lot of glitz in most people's lives back then. The Depression, you know. I had a top hat, and a cane, and a skirt that came off. Leotard underneath. Very high heels. And we had to kick high, and do a backbend over our partner's knees. It was a strenuous number.

Don was my partner. He used to wait till the curtain fell, then tickle me. Or move his knee, suddenly. I had to be on guard. Some of those curtains, in small-town theatres, were pretty flimsy. We couldn't move till the stage lights were off and the house lights on.

Did I mention Betty? She became my best friend. You needed a best friend. A best friend was very useful. Someone to watch your back, get you out of sticky situations. Lie to the manager for you. Oh, I'm just kidding about that. Betty and I got together because we both thought all of the other girls were idiots. Some of them really were! Well. I don't know. Developmental problems, you'd say nowadays. I'm not saying feeble-minded. They had to be able to play orchestra music, and dance and sing. But maybe they had been sickly as children and didn't go to school. Or maybe they were kept home, because of their size. One girl said that she hadn't gone to school because they couldn't get shoes small enough to fit her feet! I don't know if that was true.

Some were bright enough, but silly. I guess that's what Betty and I meant, when we said they were idiots. They were silly girls. All they thought about was falling in love. They spent hours talking about what kind of engagement rings they might get.

And they took themselves too seriously, as showgirls. Panics and piques all day long. Betty and I were not like that. We thought it was a fun way to make some money so we could go on with our real lives. Betty was saving up for university, to study engineering. And she did, too – she helped design planes, during the war. She said being little gave her a different perspective on the spatial relationships of things.

Me, I just wanted to put a roof over my head. Well, I wanted to provide enough so that my mother wouldn't sell our house, as she was threatening to. And I was right to do that, because I inherited the house and I'm still living in it. Yes! This is the house. Now isn't it a nice house? I've lived here since I was born, except when I was travelling. I've never wanted to live anywhere else. I got my fill of variety, travelling around Canada and the States for six years.

Novelty! That's what we were, a novelty. Mr. Berger – he was our impresario – wasn't a little person. He'd had a son who was, though. Or so they said. He wanted to showcase that talent comes in small packages. That was the official line, the one he gave in interviews. Really, I think he was one of those people who has an obsession to make something out of the imagination. He had a vision of a perfect performing troupe of tiny people, and he made it. He was always driving us to be better. He hired dancing teachers that just punished us, I can tell you. None of us were professional to start but you couldn't tell, after a year. Scare people enough and you can make them do anything. Well, I guess that was the lesson of the 30s. Hey?

Yes, Mr. Berger was a dictator. But he paid us well. And he *made* us.

Oh, we went everywhere. I saw Florida, Alabama, Georgia, Texas. Idaho, Kansas, Indiana. All of New England. I liked the big southern cities best, myself. Miami, Houston, New Orleans. Loved those! I loved being warm. I weighed eighty pounds – I was always cold. I loved New York in winter, though. The lights. Always something new to see. I liked it all.

We travelled by train. When we got off we were protected by hired policemen. They walked us to our taxis. We weren't to go out alone. We had to control our deportment in public – no getting drunk and so on. I had less freedom than I'd had at home! That was a good joke on my mother.

Who came to our shows? Well, everyone with a dollar to spare. We were family entertainment. Sometimes – I'll tell you this, now – sometimes certain gentlemen came asking for a private show. Just some of the girls, they wanted. Dancers. Mr. Berger always said no. But I think some of the more foolish girls set up private engagements. What did they want, those men? Some said it was paedophilia, but I don't think so. We were all real women, developed, you now. I think they must have seen us more like *dolls*. It was just an extension of what our audience wanted from us. They wanted to see a copy of something familiar, but reduced to a manageable size. That was it.

The smaller girls, that's who they wanted. Jeannie Lyons, now – she got flowers and cards with phone numbers all the time. She was under four feet and normally proportioned, mostly, though I think her legs were a little bit short. She wore really high heels that had to be custom-made. She wore a child's size nine shoe, if I remember. She was pretty. Big eyes, curls, pouty lips that were the fashion then. Maybe her face was a little flat. Maybe she was a little curvy, a little plump. It's hard to keep your weight down, when you're that short. Oh, Jeannie, she was very popular. And she went out, too – Mr. Berger couldn't stop that. She went out with a friend as chaperone, that was the rule, but the friend was paid to sit in a bar by herself.

The men who liked Jeannie, you know – they were not small men. They were always taller than average. Older. Well-off.

I never did understand that.

Oh, yes. Don was supposed to be my boyfriend. Or my fiancé. That was, or started out as, a ruse. There was a man who started coming to the stage door, asking for me. This was in Pittsburgh. He followed us to the next city and the next. Always at the stage door: It was tedious. Betty told me I should say I already had a boyfriend, so I did. Then, he wanted to meet my boyfriend. So I roped in Don – he was always up for a laugh. Don said, *Why don't you make it fiancé? That'll scare him off.* So then I said we were engaged.

You have to understand, the press wrote about us. We were like the Dionne quints – we had no privacy. People could find out almost anything they wanted about us.

It was in the papers. Little Couple Ties Knot. And that was annoying. But then Don, my so-called fiancé, who had always been the joker, the life of the party, got all serious. I don't just mean about me – I mean about everything. He went sour. Criticized everything, wouldn't go out. I guess being a fiancé was making him miserable! He couldn't see that, though. When I tried to break it off, he grew more morose. He was making plans to leave the company, find a job in Winnipeg – that's where he was from. And getting more controlling every minute. I wasn't to do this; I wasn't to hope for that. He'd always treated me like a chum, but now he wouldn't listen to me at all. Every time I opened my mouth, he told me I was wrong. Finally, I had to get Mr. Berger to speak to him, tell him it wasn't on, never had been on.

Oh, he was sore for few days. But he got over it.

What is it about us, hey? What we think we have to become.

Well, I did marry, in my forties. And I married a man who had been married twice before. Both times his wife had died. And he had been in the army. So he knew something about what he wanted, too. Not that we didn't have arguments. But the arguments were the kind we could both see around. They didn't swallow us up.

I forgot: There was something I wanted to say about Jarvis. That visit. He sort of sheep-dogged me out of the group, into the kitchen, and he said, *Go ahead, Pearl. Turn on the tap. Try the stove.* And they were all the perfect height for me: He'd had all of the fittings custom-made, about three-quarters size. Oh, it was amazing. *It's all yours,* he said. And I said, *Oh, Jarvis. I don't want to live in a* little *house.* I've thought about that many times, later. Why did I say that?

It was months later that Jarvis shot himself, though.

But I'm still here. I've still got the house I bought for my mother. Isn't that silly. Travelled all over this continent and ended back here.

I've had to do the kitchen over.

But isn't it a nice house? Look out the window. You can see a bit of the ocean, there, and the city spread out like the whole world.

It's too big a house, isn't it, for one little person like me. But everything is just where it should be. It hasn't let me down, this house.

ECHOLOCATION

THE DOCTOR'S ASSISTANT SAYS her bladder needs to be full for the ultrasound and keeps urging her to drink little plastic cupsful of water, so by the time Marina gets to the radiology lab, she is bursting. She can't think beyond it; the discomfort is wholly distracting. It's as though her mind is buoyed at the surface, while underneath things shift and swirl murkily. *Focus*, she commands herself, but her mind only bobs in its uppermost layers as she shifts and turns in the metal chair in the corridor. Her mind will not contemplate the implications of what is happening inside her.

Her thoughts drift instead to her daughters, ages three and five, still asleep when she left for her early morning appointment. She pictures them in their bed, facing each other like vertical bookends: in the upper bunk, the older child curled facedown, clutching a tangle of quilt, and in the lower bunk, her younger sister sprawling face-up, arms outspread across her pillows. A perfect pair, Steve always says. Why take chances?

Later this morning, when Steve has gone to work, the three of them will walk down the streets to the fresh-air market to buy food for the party she and Steve are giving tonight. Brown with the ripeness of summer, the girls will walk ahead of her, squabbling amicably, tumbling into sudden exclusive consensus as they choose the purple onions and aubergines, the yellow and red bell peppers. They have assumed her baskets, her migratory routes among the favourite stalls, the counting of leftover change to see if there's enough for *pain au chocolat*. Yes, self-sufficient, they appear.

Only she knows the rituals she has given them have bound them to her with invisible cords. Small rituals, small pleasures. An expedition to the market, with her children, in the slow time of a late August morning. How carefully she is building their lives. How she can see the whole, an image like a painting or a movie; how she has worked, one piece at a time.

Marina's name is called, and she is shown into a small cubicle – dark, full of machines and glowing green, the inside of a submarine. Her sundress pulled up above her belly. The chair reclines, like at the dentist's. The same sensation of helplessness. Supine, there's some relief of the pressure on her bladder.

The technician – soft-voiced, serious – busy with her machines. Jelly, its sticky feel; the urge to clean it off, to lick one's self like a cat. Then the paddle, a moving pressure. The technician does not look at it, but keeps her eyes on a monitor. She types; the screen changes. Nothing else happens, for a while.

In the quiet, in the darkness, her thoughts finally begin to drift and settle downward. She is conscious now of submerged fears and doubts. What if. What if. Steve's displeasure: visible. An accident. Which she would have welcomed? Would welcome?

Only the messages have not been good. The signs. And how to feel.

How long will this take, this mapping of her internal sea? And all the while, the earth's rotation changing everything irrevocably.

The paddle moves, uncomfortably, over her full bladder. It's sending and receiving sound waves that translate shape and movement into lines on the monitor. Movement into sound into image. A metaphor for something, but the metaphor is murky.

The technician touches keys, and the monitor reflects green onto her face. The glow dims and brightens as she types, bringing up successions of screens. In a moment now she will swivel the screen toward Marina and point out the finning motion, the message from inner space. Any time now. Any time now.

But the technician just keeps scrolling through new screens, and in the green glow her lips tighten.

This does not look good. But then, Marina has suspected, has sensed absence, for some days now. There have been ominous signs. There has been a silence at the end of the line.

The technician puts the paddle aside abruptly and slides off her stool. I have to see my boss, she says, pushing through the heavy curtain.

They have not told anyone, yet. Steve will say that this is fortunate, if it turns out to be bad news. *It's a good thing we haven't told the kids/our parents/our friends.* Is it a good thing, though? She understands that the silence is meant to be some sort of protection, but she suspects that she is not the beneficiary of it. She does not feel safe at all.

Now the radiologist yanks the curtain open and walks into the cubicle, trailing the technician. He has glasses, a trimmed beard. He glances at the screen, grunts, and leaves again without meeting Marina's eyes. Bad news. Bad news. The technician follows him out. Through the curtain Marina can hear them whisper. The words are not distinct but the tone is harsh. What? What? But then she understands. They are arguing.

Yes. That is it. The technician returns, tight-lipped, to deliver what must be a set speech about policy and Marina having to wait until her doctor contacts her with the results.

She does look at Marina now. In her expression, sympathy. It is not the technician's fault, of course; it is the inflexibility of the system that will sentence her. She will not take their sympathy. She won't let them snag her with their hooks of sympathy. As long as they can't reach her, she's still safe.

It doesn't look good, does it? she asks, trying to sound casual, detached. And then, to make things easier on the technician, asks, mock-plaintively, if she can pee now.

No, it doesn't look good, the technician admits. She asks Marina if she has anyone with her and directs her to the washroom, gravely.

Marina has to read the instructions on the parkade meter three times, but at last she figures it out. It's a new machine, completely automated. It reads her ticket, calculates how long she's been parked and how much money she owes, accepts her coins and validates the ticket. All without a single human presence.

STEVE'S WIFE IS WEARING a red dress, which makes her easy to spot as she swims through their guests. It's an off-red, or orangey red, the same shade, now that he thinks of it, as the spikes of flowers standing on the table, the red fishy bits on some of the hors d'oeuvres. It's a sexual colour, vaguely disturbing. Her red dress fits her sleekly, her brown arms and legs are slim and firm.

The doctor's phone call this morning had come before Marina had returned from the clinic. For some reason, the clinic couldn't tell Marina the results of her ultrasound directly. So by the time Marina was climbing the steps, he was already rehearsing what he should say. Not knowing if she knew or not, afraid of her unhappiness. In the end, the words had unreeled involuntarily from his tongue: Should we cancel the party tonight? And she had shaken her head without looking at him. No, she had answered. I don't see the point of cancelling now; it would be more trouble than going ahead, wouldn't it? He had been relieved, had put his arms around her, but she had slipped away, running past him up the stairs.

He had found her later, sitting between their two daughters, watching cartoons on TV. The children both had their bare feet in her lap, and she was holding onto them, her wrists crossed, her thumbs and forefingers encircling their ankles, so that the three of them formed a kind of complicated, continuous loop.

Now he watches her, the red dress flickering among the grazing guests. He sees her replenishing drinks, rescuing the stranded (but not getting snagged herself), smiling, nodding, accepting compliments on the food, the décor. She says she does not like to give parties, but she is good at them. She makes them look effortless: this afternoon, dicing the bright vegetables, shredding the salmon and crab, filling the flimsy pastry shells, the phyllo leaves, with a rhythmic delicate touch. She had brought red gladioli from the market that pick up the colour of her dress. He had watched her slipping her new linen shift over her shoulders, tiny gold hoops into her earlobes.

He had stood behind the half-closed ensuite door and watched her. She does not like being watched as she dresses.

He does not like parties. Does not like the day skewed to prepare, the conversations that change direction as if from some invisible signal, the morning-after flotsam of bottles and dishes and paper napkins.

He does not like that at their parties she slips by him without seeing him. Or without seeming to see him. What does he want? she always asks. He doesn't know. He doesn't know what he has the right to ask for.

Later in the evening, he meets her in the kitchen. She looks tired, preoccupied, but gathers herself into alertness when she notices him.

How are you doing? he asks, setting empty bottles down on the counter. She smiles distantly, a flicker of movement behind her eyes.

Fine.

And then catches her breath, grips the edge of the counter.

Marina?

I'm having these contractions, that's all.

Something like a chill or a drop of pressure inside him. We should have cancelled the party. You should be at the hospital, he cries out.

Don't panic, she says, coldly. Nothing's going to happen for a while.

He watches her, listens to the clatter of the party swelling beyond the kitchen doors, tries to make a rational assessment.

There would be so much explanation if Marina were to leave the party now.

She sounds calm and she must know her own body.

He will relax; he will follow her lead.

And so he exits the kitchen silently in her wake, and for an hour, half-submerges himself in the conversations flowing around him. He watches Marina gliding among the guests in her red dress, pausing, inclining her dark head to smile her closed, self-contained smile.

He should have insisted that they do the D. and C. right away. He doesn't like things being unplanned, out of control. He shouldn't have let her be so casual this morning, telling her doctor on the phone that she'd rather wait a few days, let nature take its course. He had questioned her decision, but she hadn't budged.

Well, he won't argue any more. She is tougher than she looks.

But when he catches up with her again, as she's coming out of the bathroom, he sees that she is very pale, her lips a vivid red. She presses her spine against the door frame, closes her eyes.

All right? he asks, feeling stupid.

Of course, she says, looking up at him like a cornered animal.

He feels now that he must send out little invisible lines, little inaudible beeps in her direction, trying to sound her state. If he makes the wrong move, she will curl in on herself and he will have lost her. It's an uneasy voyage: He must know what it is that is expected of him in order to reach her, but he must not be discovered negotiating this knowledge.

When, just after the last guest has departed, she makes a final limp and clammy exit from the bathroom, he is wary, careful. He fouls up anyway.

It's all over, she says. I'm going to bed. Do you think you could put anything perishable into the fridge? I'll clean up in the morning.

He grasps the important line. What do you mean, over? he asks. Are you sure? He means, is she sure that she's alright, that nothing more needs to be done, but she misinterprets him, retreats. Oh, don't worry; it's gone, she says, coldly, flatly. I felt it pass. It's gone.

And he feels a shock, a dull blow, as she has meant him to.

IT ISN'T, OF COURSE, OVER. Two hours later, Marina is lying on a gurney in emergency, gently and inexorably hemorrhaging. An hour or so passes. The resident strolls in and various procedures are discussed. Nobody seems very worried. The specialist has been called, is on her way. All decisions are deferred until her arrival. A nurse comes in every fifteen minutes or so to take Marina's blood pressure and take away the blood-soaked surgical pads. There's a warm ocean flowing out from between her legs, but it feels purifying. All stress is leaving her body.

When she can no longer feel her lips and the edges of her thoughts start to disappear, as if someone is moving from room to room shutting off lights, she is amused and intrigued. This is very interesting, she thinks. All the extraneous matter is being shut down, and I will soon discover what is at my core. It occurs to her that she will likely die if somebody doesn't do something, but she isn't frightened, only diverted.

Then Steve leans into her line of vision (for the edges of the room have started to go black) and speaks to her. She has to concentrate very hard on what he is saying; her sense of hearing, or rather of making sense of what she is hearing, is also fading. She smiles at him tenderly. He has been taking such good care of her tonight and he must be worried. How good he is to her! How good and gentle. It's not accurate that everything goes dark. Or that there's a tunnel, or white light, though perhaps she hasn't gone far enough to have that experience.

A lightening, an enlightenment. Things float through her mind and she absolutely doesn't attach. She feels herself smile, Buddha-like, at Steve's blurry half-moon face, watches his eyes widen, his focus snap taut.

Oh, no you don't, he says.

The room gets busy. She is tilted head down, and although she has been wrapped in warmed blankets, she is shaking with cold. There are IV needles in the backs of both of her hands and four clear bags of someone else's blood have been stacked between her feet. The room is full: More nurses have come, and the gynecologist, a tiny South Asian woman, is suddenly in the room, snapping on gloves. She crackles with energy. She squeezes Steve's shoulder, pats Marina's knee, explains that there is some placenta remaining, that this is causing the bleeding. Everything will be all right, she says. A little operation. Right away nurses start to lift and adjust her, moving around her in tight choreography, and the anesthetist introduces himself, deadpanning, I'm going to knock you out.

The lights are too bright and everything is too busy.

Steve is encouraged to walk alongside the gurney as it is wheeled toward the operating room. He grips her hand very tightly and neither of them speaks. Marina thinks, for once we are on the same wavelength. We are not connected, but for now we have found a workable mode of being. She wants to convey this to Steve but can't think of a way to, with all of the people pushing her so quickly.

We are not going to make it, she thinks, weightlessly, without sadness or rancour. She sees in her mind's disembodied clarity two vessels or creatures, it doesn't really matter which, that have gone out in the dark water and lost each other. She sees that at times no communication is possible, that all these crafts or beings can manage is the sending out of oblique signals, which may or may not be decipherable on their return. There is no advantage in travelling together, in the long run. Whatever comfort or strength comes out of their occasional synchronization is undermined by the danger that they'll collide, dent and scupper each other, throw each other off course. Even the sending and receiving of the almost inaudible sounds is pointless at best, and often perilous, for misheard, distorted, the signals confuse and misdirect.

They would probably be better off on their own.

She has always privately believed that she has known precisely the instant of her conceptions, though she has never spoken of this belief to anyone else. Felt a kindling, an effervescence. Once, a shower of light and a choir, sweet and pitched almost out of her range of hearing (though that time had come to nothing, too). But there had always been a presence, a voice inside her, clear, comfortable, not trying to break through anything. Not distorted by layers of defensive mechanisms, just *there*.

Already her children are muffled to her, though she listens, though she unwraps her own layers and listens to them with her nerve endings open and waving in the dangerous air.

She wakes as she is wheeled into Recovery, and there is Steve waiting for her, reaching for her hand, tugging her back, willy-nilly, into his current.

Her tongue is a dead, leathery thing, but she needs to wet her lips.

First time we've been out together without the children in five years, she says.

His smile is too relieved, too surprised, too grateful. Something hurts her. But she will shut it off, she will close off that site, she will fly only the disarming flags, she will wait.

She will dismantle and wait, until the signal flickers through again, the flutter of inquiry, the secret reaching pulse.

THE SWIFT FLIGHT OF DATA INTO THE HEART

IT'S ONLY A HALF-HOUR DRIVE into the city on a Sunday morning, but Glen and I end up having three arguments by the time we get to my parents' apartment. I say this to my mother, in the language of my childhood, as we come in, after she kisses Glen and the girls on the cheeks, and then finally gets to me.

Never mind, she says. She doesn't ask, and I don't tell her any more.

My parents do not ever criticize Glen, nor offer space in which I may do so. Once, I started to tell my mother about something childish, thoughtless, he had done.

"If you start to notice every small thing," my mother said, staring me down with her granite-coloured eyes, "your marriage will become a war."

I notice, though, that when the girls and I visit without Glen, when he is not with us of a Sunday, my parents are more relaxed. Their old friends are more likely to drop by. They forget to speak English.

My parents live now in a similar-sized apartment to the one I grew up in, but a distinctly North American apartment, which is to say there are a lot of windows, a lot of carpeting and appliances. The walls and floors are dressed with deep-coloured, intricately patterned drapes and rugs like we had at home, and the dark furniture, with its heavy carving, its solid lines, is like the furniture of my childhood. My father has filled the glassed-in balcony with tropical plants of all kinds, so that their sliver of ocean view is strained through a garden. My mother says that my father is trying to recreate our villa at the coast. My father says my mother has tried to replace, molecule by molecule, our apartment in Sarajevo.

Glen finds it fussy, claustrophobic. Thrift-store tacky, he says, but he's mistaken about that; he's confusing my parents' heavily-patterned Venetian drapes, the beaten-silver bowls and jugs, the Turkish rugs, the carved Bosnian table legs, with pastiche versions, which are all he's ever seen. Glen likes things to have straight lines, to be straightforward, a little simple.

Because it's my father's birthday, some of our relatives have come – my father's two sisters, small, olive-skinned women in head scarves and severe grey wool coats, Aunty Mirash and Aunty Bobia, and the husband of one of them, Uncle Sevo, who wears layers of cardigans and has stained yellow grey moustaches that hang below his chin. They scold me in a dialect of their language, which I don't really understand anymore, or don't try to understand.

They're kind of scary-looking; Damira avoids them, and Ally won't even look at them. Naturally, they want to maul the children. I have to say that Glen is good at defending the girls from their advances. They seem afraid of Glen, who's a good foot taller than any of them, and can assume an impressive formality. I am ashamed to say that even I hide behind Glen, in the face of my aunts' intensity, their vociferous-sounding utterances, their dark thick clothing and smells. But I am not too ashamed. I notice even my mother does this: She defers to Glen when the aunts are in her house, as if to say, What can I do? Here is this tall, serious English Canadian who will not approve.

Out of my aunts' hearing, my mother complains – about their refusal to learn English, to dress normally, to buy their halal chickens at Superstore, which they can get to on the bus, rather than demanding that my father drive them out to Surrey.

They don't even eat halal all the time, my mother scolds, her round eyes owl-like behind her thick glasses. My father doesn't keep his family's religion, and my mother isn't of his ethnic background. My parents are both educated, professionals, and consider religion in the same way, perhaps, as Glen thinks of their taste in furniture.

There's another visitor, too – they've brought another man with them, this time. His name is Josip, and he's just come out from Toronto. He's a friend or relative of my parents: someone from the old life. Like all of us, he immigrated between ten and fifteen years ago, but my parents haven't seen him till now.

There is a lot of that: reunions of people who left in a hurry, in chaos, often with very little. Now that they have found their feet, feel safe to move around, have learned some English, use the internet, they are finding each other again, they are coming together, coalescing, reforming their communities.

There's a lot of conversation in Bosniak, in spite of Glen's presence, today. I can't follow all of it. And then a call from the States, from my brother Paval, who talks more to our mother, though it's our father's birthday. My mother says, He's got a new girlfriend! And my father says, He's bought a new car! A Porsche, this time. The aunts and uncle ruminate on the news. *Porsche* is the only word I can understand.

Josip makes an attempt in English: Paval, he says, is a playboy. We all smile.

My father says, Paval is a boy still. He does not settle. He doesn't take responsibility.

He left something behind, when you came to Canada, Josip says. He left behind the knowledge of how to become a man. It was in the soil, the mountains, the trees, you see.

Pshaw, my mother says. We have lived in the city for five generations. And Paval has a great job; he's very successful. Why should he settle down yet? He's barely thirty.

And what did I leave behind, Papa? I ask, beneath the rest of the conversation. By which I mean, Where am I broken? And I both long for and dread his answer. But he only pats my hand. Why, you are missing nothing, he says. You have made a good life. You have made everything one could wish for one's children.

I feel so terribly depressed when he says this.

We eat my mother's spicy lamb stew, mopping our plates with the spongy flatbread that Glen refers to as sour pancakes. Damira won't eat any of it; she claims it's funny-tasting, too spicy, stinky. But she has eaten this dish happily before. It's the breakfast sandwich Glen bought her on the way here that has changed her mind, and things she's heard Glen say. The aunts scold in whispers about Damira pushing her food away. Ally, sitting on a riser of two telephone books next to my father, eats a surprising amount. My father has figured out some-how that she will eat if she is given a teaspoon of everything on a plate, the bits of food carefully separated. How does he know this? So there is a little mound of rice, a mound of stew, a mound of vegetables in sauce. Damira asks, what kind of meat is this? My mother is about to say, lamb, and my father cuts in: Just meat, dear. But Damira won't eat it, anyway.

Glen eats a good helping. Later, I think, he'll complain about the heaviness of the meal. He is getting a little fat, but it is not my mother's cooking that is making him so.

AFTER, WE ALL WALK through the park, slowly, except Glen who has stayed behind to watch some sort of sports on the little television set in the den. The aunts and uncle and Josip walk ahead, sombrely, exotically. My mother and I keep pace, making conversation about my possible kitchen renovation – my mother has lots of opinions, which I try to respond to politely – and my father walks with the girls, who stop and examine the things that small children examine in parks. My mother and I turn around to wait for them. They have on parkas, as it's November, and the wind already chilly, damp.

Damira's parka is black, with fur on the hood. At five, she has already a sense of her own image; she likes to wear black, which my mother deplores. But it sets off Damira's strawberry-blonde hair, her pale skin. Ally is darker, with brown hair and my father's almond-shaped black eyes. She has darker skin and hair than I do, even. She's a throwback. She's wearing Damira's old blue parka, which isn't her colour. My mother says: That's not Ally's colour. She should have red. I'll buy her a red coat. But I know that Ally will not accept a change; she doesn't like change, and the burden that I carry around, the burden of Ally's emerging difficultness, makes me feel anxious, so I say, It's fine, mother. Don't always be so critical.

My father walks toward us, my two daughters holding his hands. They stop before crossing one of the park roads, waiting for traffic to go by, and I see, suddenly, that my father is getting old, and that my daughters are very small and not at all safe to be out in the world by themselves. I can see my mother thinking the same thought.

Then Josip drops back to walk with my parents, with the air of someone who has very gallantly done his social duty and can now relax and enjoy himself. My parents press him for news of relatives, acquaintances. It's very tedious to listen to, but my parents are a node, a connection, for a lot of other people. Their interest is necessary.

Our family was lucky: We left in good time. My parents had connections, they got immigration papers, were able to transfer the bulk of their money into Canada. Both are university professors (retired now), in fields in which language was not a big barrier, in fields where there was demand. I hear all of the time of former doctors, engineers, lawyers, who work as janitors, busboys, drivers. My parents found new jobs at a university within a year of our landing here.

It was as if they were able to pick us up, pick up our entire lives, and set them down in a new continent, a new city. It was as if we lost nothing, except for our house by the sea. All the terrible things that happened in our country did not happen to us, you understand. Words like *genocide, tank, mass grave*, are not much more familiar to us than they are to the average Canadian who watches the news. My parents tell us how lucky we are, how we must not look back.

Perhaps lucky isn't the right word.

My parents were reading the papers. They had read the history books. A teacher asked my brother, at school, about the ethnicity of his surname. My parents read the signs, and decided to leave. They were right to do so. Probably. No, not probably. There have been reports from former neighbours, relatives. And all of the news, of course. Things would not have gone well for our family.

They acted intelligently, and were saved. But now they must pay; I think in their own minds they are paying, by first of all helping so many others who have come over, and second, never ceasing to remind Paval and me of the necessity of prudence.

AND THEN, as we are strolling through the park, Josip mentions a name I haven't heard in a long time. It's the name of my mother's cousin, and also the mother of someone I used to know. I begin to listen. I listen as a blind man might listen, preparing to cross a street. This woman, this cousin of my mother's, has perhaps died, or rather, her sister-in-law has died. Josip was at the funeral, and talked to this woman, who asked about my mother.

And I ask, in my somewhat rusty mother tongue (but as casually as I can manage) if the woman's son, my old acquaintance, was at the funeral too.

No, no, Josip answers. But you see Alex, eh? Here in Vancouver? You like his restaurant?

Which restaurant? Which restaurant? I wait for my parents to ask, or to confirm they knew this, or express surprise, but they are already talking about something else.

Which restaurant? I ask. Josip scratches his head, rubs his fingers together, makes a disgusted sound. Can't remember. Just slipped my mind.

This is a good-sized city. There are hundreds of restaurants. Thousands, perhaps. And when someone says *his restaurant*, do they mean the place he owns, or the place in which he busses tables, washes dishes? And when they say restaurant, do they mean tables with linen covers, or a street kiosk?

MY FATHER HAS CLEVERLY KEPT a surprise for the girls, which is necessary to get them to walk back to the apartment. Even so, Ally has to be carried the last few blocks. My mother carries her, on her shoulders: She says my father's back has been bad lately. They will never let me carry her, and Ally won't be touched by anyone outside the family.

The surprise is that my father has bought a cage and a pair of very small finches, which are kept in the glassed-in balcony.

I remember that he kept finches at our villa by the sea, and that they flew around the house. Yes, says my mother, spreading their seed and droppings everywhere. My father says that they will only fly around the sunroom, here, and that they must stay in their cage for a few days, to get used to it, before they are let out.

The girls are entranced, of course. We have no pets; Glen is allergic to anything with fur or feathers. The little finches look painted, with daubs of bright russet and black and white, and beaks of an artificial-looking orange. They are tiny, cheerful-seeming. They trill with a sort of electronic sound, a buzz. They flit and trill around their little cage, as if they're happy there. We're all very happy with the little finches.

Glen says to me, as we are leaving, You seem kind of spaced. You're not really paying attention.

My mother says: We walked too far. We're all tired.

MY MOTHER IS TAKING ME to lunch and shopping. It is my birthday week: I am turning thirty-three. Glen will look after the girls, of course, my mother says. When I stop by the office where she does her volunteer work, three days a week, she is still busy. The woman who comes out of her cubicle, finally, has fine, coffee-coloured skin, the cheekbones and lips of a princess, the posture of someone who is used to wearing a crown. She gives me a haughty look, and I give her one back. My mother complains about her, at lunch. She left the documents she needs at home. Then she tells me about the woman's husband's sudden death, her sister's, aunt's, brother's. All in a year. Her three children, not enough to eat. They're not doing so well, she says.

I am a refugee, I say.

What? my mother says, sounding shocked.

I am a refugee. A citizen, of course, with an education, a profession, a house, a car. But still a refugee. Every day, I am conscious of the space my body takes up in this city: That space seems borrowed, loaned, temporary.

When we arrived, my father said: Look at all of this space! This country has room for you to become anything you can imagine. My brother Paval turned his Walkman louder, made himself small in the corner of the back seat of the taxi. I understood that. We didn't want more possibilities, more of the unknown. We wanted our familiar lives back, and if that was not possible, we wanted our new lives to be small, safe, predictable as they had never really been.

I took English as a Second Language classes. I went to university. I applied for a job on a women's magazine. I did the work I was asked for, and some extra. I was promoted. I got married and gave birth to two children. All in a dream, it seems now.

I was married in my parents' living room: I wore a grey wool suit, expensive, but not new. My job interview suit. Only my immediate family, Glen's parents and sisters, and their spouses, were invited. Afterwards, we all drove in our own cars to a good restaurant, where we had booked a room for a *table d'hôte* luncheon. My father paid for the luncheon. There was wine, but not champagne: my idea. Glen was pleased that the wedding didn't cost too much, wasn't complicated to arrange. But there: I am unfair. I wanted dignity, a minimum of fuss. I do not remember what else I thought or felt that day. I do remember there was rain, and that I carried a small bouquet of some forced white flower. In photographs, I look like a model in a bridal fashion magazine: like someone pretending to be a bride, for the sake of the dress.

I'm a good wife, I think. I don't complain or criticize. I cook the foods my husband likes. I keep an orderly house, mind the children. I stick to a budget; I contributed to the mortgage and RRSPs, when I was working. I see the movies my husband wants to see. I never turn down sex. I know from reading magazines, and from overhearing lunch time conversations, that these are the things husbands complain about.

All of this is easy. I have no patience with women who can't manage a job, a house, a marriage, children, competently. It's not rocket science, as they say.

The trick is not to care about any of it too little, or too much.

That is what I mean by *refugee*.

After lunch, the shopping in smart Yaletown, trying on clothes by local designers, beautiful coats like priest's robes, in cashmere and mohair, draped so perfectly that they are like origami. They suit Mother well, with her tall, angular frame, her sharp cheekbones. I love them: I am in love with these coats. I want one of them especially, an asymmetrical fall of earth-coloured cashmere, more than anything else I've ever seen. But it, like the others, is scaled much too long for me. I look like a hobbit. The salesgirl says it can be hemmed shorter, but she says it doubtfully. We all know that the entire premise is too big for me.

We will find something for you here, she says, leading me to another shop. I see little Asian ladies go here all the time, she says. The coat is grey silk; it is the kind of expensive silk that does not shine, but seems itself a source of light. It is fitted, with a high waist and a stiff, round collar, like a little girl's dress. I do not like it, but Mother says, Try it on, and when I do it turns me into something – a china princess, I think – in its stiffness, and Mother buys it for me, and I do not resist.

Now you are a grown woman, you need some good clothes, Mother says. I imagine Damira and Ally putting their sticky hands on the silvery silk. I hope that I will not scold them when they do.

My mother is a formidable woman. She was celebrated in her field, and now that she is retired, she volunteers a full three days a week, and still looks after all of us. She will take anything on. Yet I have always felt in her a barely concealed panic toward me, a sense that she finds me too difficult, too confusing to deal with. We almost always end up talking about clothes.

MY BROTHER PAVAL is a rocket scientist: He works for NASA. Our parents complain, mildly, under their pride, that they never see him. He is always busy. I imagine his life: a few select friends, his perfect industrial-minimalist apartment, his new Porsche. His time structured as carefully as one of the computer models he makes.

Our parents talk about his busyness with pride and longing. He has removed himself, a little, from our orbit.

We celebrate his birthday without him: our parents and I, my daughters.

WHEN MY DAUGHTER ALLY WAS BORN, Paval came to visit me. This was a surprise; he was still a student, but had already begun to evade the net of family conventions. Perhaps my mother had said something, in some sort of fright, to him on the telephone: It had been a difficult, fraught birth, at one point dangerous for both Ally and me. Now I lay in a hospital bed, wounded, exhilarated. Paval picked Ally up from her transparent plastic bassinet, held her up like she was some new electronic device. I swear he turned her over, as if to read her specifications.

Interesting, he said, and put her back in the bassinet. Then leaned on the window ledge, looked at me. Your eyes are all bruised and your lips are cracked and swollen, he said. Is that normal?

Thanks, I said. My hair felt dirty and my abdominal muscles hurt so that I couldn't even roll over, and I thought I probably smelled bad.

I heard some interesting news, my brother said. Alex S...., you know, our cousin, he used to visit us at our summer house – he's alive, after all. He's in Canada. He was captured, it seems, and in a prison camp, but then he escaped and lived in the hills for a while, made his way out of the country, ended up in Montreal, somehow, without papers.

For the second time that week, my heart almost stopped.

WE WERE AT OUR VACATION HOUSE on the seacoast. (It was the first thing to be lost, to be taken, the vacation house. Along with everything kept in it.) I was sixteen, my brother Paval thirteen. Pav had a motorbike, a small one. I rode it:

I did not know how to ride, but I got on, gunned it, flew down the hill, the sea glinting almost white over my right shoulder, my hair whipping around my neck. At the foot of the hill: you in an ancient car. You stopped, rolled down your window. I knew who you were: You had the family face, the curling upper lip. You took off your sunglasses. I saw that you had the same eyes as Pav and my mother: round, granite with squiggles of gold. You reached an arm out of the window, grabbed the handlebar of my bike.

Who are you? you asked. I saw in your face that you thought I was interesting, in a sexual way, and wild, dangerous, even.

The second day of your visit I seduced you, in the sea cave, the one we called the Glass Grotto, at the turning of the low tide. I had planned, since I was, oh, eleven or so, since I knew, more or less, about sex, to seduce someone in that grotto. It was the perfect place: the rocks razor-edged with barnacles, the pools charged with sharp-toothed eels, stinging jellyfish. The tide only ebbing out of the cave for an hour. At its return, anyone inside would be trapped by the currents, drowned and shredded. There was a small patch of damp sand, body-sized. I lay on it and pulled you over me.

You were reluctant, but I arched up my girl's breasts, put my tongue in your mouth, made you believe I knew what I was doing. Maybe I did. Oh, yes. You were twenty-two; you had a girlfriend (with you on this trip!); you were my second cousin.

You came to visit, when we were back in the city, surprising my mother. She had been fond of you when you were a small boy, but wary, later, when you grew up, when political schisms separated that branch of her family. We used subterfuge; we were guerrilla lovers. We made love in my parents' bed while they were at work (and I supposedly at school).

Then I talked my parents into letting me enrol in another university than the one at which my parents taught. A university in the city you lived in. Then you were almost living with me; we saw each other every day.

You said: We must not be too exclusive; we must not fall in love. You said you had other girlfriends. I said I had other boyfriends, too. It did not occur to me that you might be lying.

Then the tanks in the city. My parents sent for me in a hurry and I got on the train with my suitcases, without leaving a note for you.

I was seventeen. I didn't know yet that a careless omission, a casual mishap, will erase possibilities from life forever.

MY MOTHER HAS COOKED A DISH that is one of Paval's favourites, even though he isn't here: lamb with apricots, and an almond cake as well. We eat the meal in a relaxed, pleasant way. My father puts Ally's food in the little compartments on her plate. Damira eats without a fuss, partly because Glen is not present. My parents telephone Paval, and Ally gets to talk to him as well. She chatters about the birds, the adored birds.

The little finches, it seems, have done well. They have produced two tiny eggs, pea-sized eggs, but perfectly white and oval, in a tiny nest. They sing: *zee zee*, their little computer sound. Their little painted bodies flit around their cage. Damira wants to see them fly, but my father says they are too nervous, with extra people in the house. They must be peaceful, they must be protected, to hatch those eggs.

But later, somehow, the cage is opened (we suspect Ally, but it could have been Damira, who can't leave the birds alone) and the mother bird escapes and flaps, panicky, into the light fixtures, the curtain headers. She takes refuge, briefly, on top of the kitchen cabinets, and my father climbs up on a stool to catch her, but as he extends his hand, the bird flies away again, trilling in alarm or defiance. My father moves, slowly, calmly; he almost catches her, a few times, but she keeps slipping away. Then he stops: We'll leave the door to the balcony open, he says, and she will settle down. And she does, the little bird, after a few more panicked flights at the windows. She perches in one of the potted plants, and my father catches her by throwing the dishcloth over her.

But when she is put back into the cage, she doesn't perch: She sits on the floor of the cage. The other bird, the male, leaves the nest, flies around the cage.

My mother says, needlessly: the eggs will have cooled too much now.

Then the little female is dead. She resembles, even more, a painted toy. There is a little blood at her cloaca. My mother says that she must have had eggs inside still that broke when she struck the walls and window. Damira sobs; she won't be comforted. My father shouts at my mother, in their own language, that she should mind what she says, and my mother shouts back that he was foolish to bring the birds into the apartment, with little children. That is the first time that I have seen my mother and father argue since we left our old country. We are careful with each other, in my family.

SO I CARRIED THAT NEWS HOME from the hospital after Ally's birth, along with Ally, held close to my heart. Why didn't I try to contact you then? I don't know. Imagine it: me sore, battered; Damira still in diapers, Ally a difficult baby, struggling with asthma, eczema, colic, as if she'd been born into the wrong planet, into an environment hostile to her external and internal surfaces. For her first three years, I did not sleep more than a couple of hours at a time.

I did look for you, especially when the internet got better, when it could be used to find people. There are three men in Montreal with your name, four in Toronto. I couldn't call from home – Glen pays the phone bills, audits them each month; it's one of his hobbies – but I made awkward trips to the one mall I could find at which the payphones worked and the corridor was not too noisy, and I worked my way through the phone numbers, Ally in a sling on my side. It occurred to me that there were many other cities I could check, but after a time, I gave up.

But I would not have recognized you then. I would not have admitted you to my life. I was complete. No: complete is the wrong word. I lived in a vortex of busyness. The chaos of my life was enough to contain me.

And I thought that I could find you any time I wanted.

I say to my mother, as we're having tea in her gilt-edged glasses, do you and Father see much of your friend Josip? Where is he living? I say this as casually as possible, I think.

My mother says: You know that you need to go back to work now. Ally is too attached to you. With Damira in kindergarten and Alexandra three, you should go back to work.

They won't take her at the daycare, I said. She can't speak properly and she can't get the hang of the toilet. And she screams.

She's too distracted at that place, my mother says. Bring her here. Papa will watch her for you.

It's not rocket science. I think: I *do* need to go back to work. I need my days filled again; I need my name on the editorial page again.

Yes, I say. I will go back to work.

A woman needs something more than cleaning her house and watching a child, my mother says. And you don't want to get too mixed up with those refugees. Some of them have so many problems that they have brought with them. They can consume your whole life.

Does she mean Josip, or someone else?

I am a refugee, I say.

My mother shakes her head, smiling fiercely. You must go back to work, she says. Even when she smiles, her eyes are very round, alarmed-looking. It feels that she is trying to give me a hidden message.

PAVAL COMES BACK for our mother's birthday, though it seems he was taking holidays then anyway. He brings her a fur coat, a real fur coat, the soft skins of some small animal, as a gift. My mother loves it. She has no compunction, it seems, about small soft animals. She makes sure that Damira and Ally have clean hands before they are allowed to stroke her. The fur is a soft grey with a kind of shadow – ombré, it is called. It floats nearly down to her ankles. Glen estimates its cost, and is sanctimonious. He underestimates by about half, too – Mother tells me, later what she insures the coat for. Glen, I can see, also feels outdone: There is no way we can match that gift. But I don't care. I have decided that my gift to my mother is to just exist. As she insists on that, she can take it as my offering. Of course, Glen and I have given her some new Le Creuset casserole dishes and a bathrobe and flowers, as well. But she and I both know, I remind myself, of what is the real gift.

Paval has also arranged for all of us to go out to dinner. Otherwise, he said, Mother will end up cooking her own birthday dinner, which is true. He wanted it to be just the seven of us, but Mother and Father have insisted that all of the hangers-on come too – they will pay for the hangers-on – and so Paval booked a whole room, *table d'hôte*. He did this, prudently, a whole month in advance, and let me know.

When I heard the name of the restaurant, I knew immediately that I had found something I was looking for.

I was back at my desk, back at my job that had been kept open for me: out of my great value, I tell myself, not out of compassion or a string of bad fits in my temporary successors. Back overseeing articles on "Ten Financial Mistakes Women Make" and "Decorating Your House for the Holidays." (We are wrapping that article this very week: Christmas features are produced in August, to be ready for October release. The photographers put blue film on the windows, when shooting interior shots of decorated mantelpieces and trees, to get a wintery light.)

I was working, and had a good computer at my disposal, and also a new cellphone, and time I did not have to account for, during the day. I received my brother Paval's email, telling me the name of the restaurant he had booked, on the weekend, and I thought: I will phone. On Monday, first thing, I will phone.

It was the first independent, active thought that I'd had in fifteen years.

But then your email, like a bird, like the great shoe-headed storks in our country that return in spring, back home winging all the way from Africa to flap heavily onto the roofs.

So that is how it feels, I thought: The open air in front of you gathers itself into a wall, and you strike it, and in your brain, an explosion of light, and then blankness.

It was so unexpected that for the first second I was confused: I thought that I might have already have called you, and the email was a reply. That you'd somehow heard I'd traced you, finally, back to this rainy city. I thought for a confused second that someone had passed on the information that I was looking for you, and that's why you had emailed me.

You had, you said, been sitting in a waiting room on the weekend. One of your cooks had cut herself. You had picked up the magazine, flipped through it. My photograph, my email address. Had said to yourself: I will email right away.

You said, you will think this strange, but I have been thinking about you. I thought I saw you near the law courts one day, on the street, in a red coat.

That kind of coincidence is disturbing. It shakes the fabric of things. It makes you think more things are possible than really are.

Now is the point where I feel it necessary to lay everything out, to make it clear that this happened, this dual firing of missiles, at the same moment. Why is that? Obviously, I feel my intent will be questioned, my motives doubted. My actions, of course. I have long ago erased the email you sent. I erased it in a great hurry without printing it out or committing it to memory, so guilty was I already.

I keep returning to the coincidence of our mutual sending up of flares, as if that coincidence removes responsibility, makes what followed inevitable. And I keep hearing a voice of reason that questions my logic. Is it my mother's voice? A voice like hers, at least: cool, rational. You have known Alex was in Canada for over three years now, the voice says. And why did Alex not email or contact you before? He must have known – through Josip, or others – that you lived here. It is not my mother, though – it is my own brain. My mother does not know these details.

When we arrive at the restaurant, seeing the name, only my father is surprised. Oh! he says. Such an odd coincidence! That was the name the children gave to that little grotto at the beach, by our summer home, wasn't it? I'd forgotten about that. Do you think there is any connection?

I notice then that my father is the only one who is innocent. My mother, my brother Paval, and I say nothing. Glen, of course, comments that the restaurant looks "dubious," but that is not out of any covert intelligence. He had tried to subvert the plans, to get my mother's birthday dinner changed to another location, for example a franchised steak house, where he "knew what he was going to get."

I feel I do not need to say this: that my mother and Paval somehow know, as if I were transparent, as if they have foreseen this for years.

THIS IS NOT A WAR STORY; I have said that. I have not said that my parents are slightly different colours than each other, and that their faces show different genetic origins very clearly. Canadians are not used to that – Canadians of European descent are all blended together, northern and southern, mountain and valley races. Even my daughters' faces show only vestiges of my father's eyelids, his lips, and no trace of their paternal great-grandmother's jutting Scottish jaw.

In my former country, there were three peoples – three main peoples. Some raped and tortured and murdered others. Some lost seaside villas. And some, at the time of this story, are being tried by an International Criminal Tribunal for war crimes. My father's and mother's families were ancient enemies, and you, in spite of your relation to my mother, were also suspect in your connections.

I have said that the war did not touch my immediate family – my mother and father, Paval and me – so closely. We lived in a bubble of protective data, and we were lucky. Others in my country did not have this fortune. When the trials were beginning to be televised, last year, Paval and I talked about them privately; we did not mention them to our parents, nor they to us. We are all careful with each other, in our family.

AT THE HUGE TABLE that has been set for us, where my mother and father sit like bride and groom, there is much happiness. It's an important birthday for my mother. She's a little older than my father, and there's a lot of teasing about her great age, her "much younger" husband. I've heard the stories, before, but listen now with new interest: my mother, in her mid-thirties, an academic, apparently devoted to her career in mathematics, shocking everyone by bringing home a younger man of a different, suspect, background. My mother says, as she always does: What could I do? He made me so happy. And my father smiles. But for the first time, maybe, I see the wickedness, the sex, in the smile. So.

My father has given my mother – or rather, they have decided together that this will be her gift – a trip for the two of them back to their country, or rather the new country that our little part of the world has become. And it is not so clear-cut: Though my family lived in one city, though I grew up there, they were both from different places, now different countries. The city where I went to university, where I almost-lived with you, that's a separate country now, as is the place on the coast where our villa was. It is not as simple as each party gaining what it wanted. There is always loss.

YOU SAY, *I want, I want.* The effect on me is of hearing the cry of a newborn: My body responds involuntarily, with a need to respond. Not mother's milk, but something else, courses in my veins.

You send an email to me at work and tell me what you will do to me: you will put your mouth here and here, on various parts of me. These parts of my body evidently can read. They send up little flares: We are here! We answer you! My brain, on the other hand, panics: I delete the message from my inbox; then delete it from trash so fast that it has hardly existed. Then I regret. I can never read it again.

You won't say I love you. You say that phrase is a commitment, not a proclamation. You do not say that you are mine exclusively. You do not mention the future.

You say: When you disappeared, it was as if you had taken a fish knife and gutted me. I know the knife you mean; we kept it at the villa, for cleaning catches. I can see it, its sharp wicked purposeful construction. I can never explain why I left without a word.

At this dinner, my mother's birthday dinner, there are all the fruits of the sea. It was not on the menu, but here it is: platters and platters of tiny clams, of cloud-soft scallops, buttery prawns, little fried octopus; then sole, salmon, tuna, swordfish, all prepared exquisitely, in the style of the Adriatic coast. Glen, who doesn't particularly like seafood, whispers, angrily: How much is this going to cost?

I straighten my shoulders. There must be a war soon, I know: I will have to start it, or it will start itself. It will be an ugly war: Each side will believe that the other is only fighting out of selfish motives. Each will accuse the other of heinous behaviour, but each will also be guilty. It will gut me out, this war. I will lose much of what is important to me.

Every barb, every irritation, then, can stiffen my resolve.

What am I to say: that I have been here twice a week for the past two months, arriving in the mid-afternoon, after the lunch service, before the evening preparation. That I know how to let myself in the side door, slip up the stairs, into the offices above the restaurant, where there is room containing only an old sofa, a sink, a toilet, and a small table with yellow legs.

Whatever I choose for my life now, I will always have that image of the table's yellow legs in my memory.

Everyone praises Paval for providing such a feast. The chef, the chef is the hero, Pav says, smiling. The chef does not appear. The platters continue to arrive. Are we recreating the Glass Grotto, or emptying the sea?

UNBEARABLE OBJECTS

THE NIGHT BEFORE, Tess had said: Please; you have to. Otherwise it'll be me. She had not been looking at him; her small head, in its knitted, striped toque, her Rasta-cap, turned away, but he knew her eyes were dangerously shiny, in her pinched little face.

If you don't do it, I'll have to, and Alison won't get her spa day, Tess said, though he knew this. Lewis has to go golfing, she said. It's not just a game; it's some executive tournament. He has to do it. It's for his *job*.

Can't argue with that. Lewis's job. No. And can't argue that Alison – poor Alison – should have a couple of hours of being pampered, that Tess should have this time with Alison, should be able to feel she is doing something good for Alison. Can't argue that he should put off what he was planning to do with his afternoon and take care of Sack.

Lying awake at six in the morning, while overhead, small heavy feet thud back and forth over hardwood and hard tile, while a child uses his definitively outside voice over and over. *I want. I want. I want.* Every goddamn morning: even weekends. And not his child, not his house. The constant reminder: He will never be able to repay them. He owes them, he is living on their charity. He has no further claim on them: not even the basic human right to sleep.

Sack has grown from a large-headed baby to, let's face it, a suburban terrorist. A monstrous child. Four years old, completely unsocialized, he careens through the house, wailing, laughing too loudly, demanding. *I want! I want!* You can't have a conversation, can't volley a sentence back without his interrupting. Lewis and Alison's social interactions are constantly fragmented by this kid, who never, never gets enough attention, and never does what he is asked, and never entertains himself quietly for fifteen minutes at a time. Lewis works, or golfs, nearly all the time. Alison has been sick since Sack was a baby. They keep him in daycare as much as possible.

Tess says, privately – her only criticism of Alison – that Sack is strung out, over-stimulated, sleep-deprived, but lacking in his parents' full attention. Do you notice, she says, they only ever tell him to be quiet, to go away? Tess is patient with Sack, tries to engage him in books and puzzles, to cuddle him, and of course he repays her by screaming at her with insane laughter and bashing at her with his big hard fists.

He and Tess haven't had children yet: won't likely, now, Tessa's ovaries having been presumably chemically fried and irradiated by her treatments.

I'll do it, he had said. And then, to make sure that Tess didn't feel sorry for him, he had leered at her, growled: But you'll owe me.

Tess had stared back at him without humour. Grow up, she had said.

Bad luck. Very bad luck, and against the odds: that is all that Matt had been able to say to his friends, his parents, when they telephoned and emailed him in concern. First Tess's sister Alison getting sick, then Matt losing his job in the aftermath of the crash. Then Tessa herself getting sick. His car accident, his fault, though there should be some exigency for when you're driving home at four in the morning after taking your dehydrated wife, who can't stop vomiting because her insides have been scorched out by the medical mafia's excuse for a cancer treatment, to emergency, and you need to be at work in three hours. The loss of his and Tess's house, subprime mortgage, of course. And Alison's recurrence, the bad news of her prognosis, just as Tess was starting to turn the corner.

Just bad luck. Misfortune. Temporary setback. No need to take it personally.

It occurs to him now that Lewis and Alison own one of those top-end jogging strollers. That Sack had been wheeled around parks in one, on visits, in the past. If Matt can find it, he will strap the little guy in it, and he can still have his run. He'll have to stick to sidewalks and chip trails, but he can still do it. He remembers that sort of harness affair, a five-point buckle. The kid won't get out of that. He can scream if he wants. Maybe he'll like it.

He will get up. He tries to move quietly, to shift his weight gradually, but Tessa is disturbed anyway. He stops moving and watches as she wakes; sees, by the sharp light entering the basement window, how, as she rises into consciousness, her face tightens. Asleep, she had looked calm, if not carefree: herself. Now, even before she opens her eyes, a vertical crease forms on her brow, and her lips pull back and thin out.

Her hair has grown out a couple of inches, and he touches it, catches one of the dark springy curls between his thumb and forefinger. It is as soft and thick as before, isn't it?

She opens her eyes, and he lets go of the tendril. Sometimes it's irritating for her to be touched.

But then she smiles, slightly, unexpectedly, and holds his gaze, and reprieve floods through him, a great gush of relief that he can't explain or name. His waking grievance is washed out now, leaving nothing but its shadowy imprint. It is not so bad. Tess is still here. They are in their own bed; their bodies fit like puzzle pieces, like keys in locks. It is not so bad. Is it?

HE HAS JUST FINISHED mowing the lawn, and has worked up a sweat. Lewis and Alison own, of course, a fashionably retro reel mower, which has to be pushed up the slopes of their half-acre lot, and which, he suspects, needs sharpening. The soft spring grass wraps itself around the spiral blades rather than suffering itself to be cleanly lopped off. It is hard going. Typical, that Lewis and Alison would plant themselves on a piece of property this ostentatious, run the furnace and/or the A/C, the washing machine, the dishwasher, the automated sprinklers, day and night, without compunction, pouring hundreds of gallons of treated, detergent-poisoned water down the sewers, and drench the lawn with toxic chemicals – and then buy a reel mower. Typical.

He wheels the mower back to the garden shed, leaving a slap of bruised green along the sidewalk. He'll have to sweep that up, too.

Tess saying to him, tiredly: You do chores like a child. Who do you think is going to finish the job for you?

His back aches; he's spent too much time sitting, lately, looking for jobs on the internet, and might as well admit it, watching clips of old TV shows on YouTube. They don't have a TV now; it's been sold. A big flat-screen HD, two years old. Had they got twenty cents on the dollar for it?

But the hills on this sunny May day stretch out around him, in their first tender green, rolling away north forever: first the deposits of suburban lots fanning along the lower reaches; then, beyond those, the golf course, mineral-green; and beyond that meadow and forest like something from a child's picture-book, clean and sparkling, a quilt of tints. He can taste in his body how it will feel to set off loping cross-country, to expand his lungs, to have the muscle-ache wake his cramped body, to drive the ground in through his foot soles.

But first he must finish the list of chores Lewis has given him, via Alison, via Tess. The complicated, stilted dance of ownership and debt and gratitude. This afternoon – and it will be sweeter for the waiting – he'll strike out across the hills, with Sack in the stroller, free for a couple of hours.

He breathes deeply, down to what Alison and Tess would call his root chakra. (He won't think about that, the amount of money a hitherto sane and logical person will spend on alternative bullshit when they are dying.) He sweeps the chewed-up grass from the sidewalk and hoses off the smears. He clips the hedge, getting into it, doing a nice symmetrical job, lacerating himself with cedar fronds. He finds the ladder, cleans out the gutters (packed with fall leaves and a bird's nest), trims the edges of the lawn where it's trying to invade the tri-coloured gravel of the shrubberies, yanks out the grass and dandelions that have insinuated themselves in-between the little pink-flowered bushes and the prickly green bushes.

He's no gardener. He had hardly been able to turn it down, though, when Tess (or Tess's and Alison's mother) had brokered the arrangement: he and Tess to live in Alison's and Lewis's basement suite in return for looking after Alison and Sack and the yard.

He hunts down the barrel where he's supposed to put the clippings and finds it half-filled with water and rotted leaves and the deadheads and stalks of flowers. Tess had come over in the fall, when they'd still been in their own house, to help Alison with the gardening. Then the barrel was abruptly abandoned, he thinks, left in the winter rain to brew a foul, slimy soup.

Where to dump something so disgusting, in a yard so manicured?

The far side of the shed, where the grass doesn't grow, where there is some soil. If he can drag the barrel there. It needs holes punched in the bottom or something. He'll do that later.

As he pours out the stinking mess, two objects more solid than the rest drop out onto the ground. He pokes them with the shovel tip: dead rats?

But then recognition: leather and cloth, blackened by mold, the fingers stuck together in what looks like an anguished clench. Gardening gloves, borrowed from Alison, last fall, and forgotten, uncharacteristically, by Tess.

That he can feel such intense, sudden pain still surprises him. He feels seared out; he imagines that the sadness and fear, the unpleasantness of the procedures, Tess's withdrawal, his deep shame at their financial predicament, have all burned out his capacity for anything other than irritation and grievance, but here is emotion again, waiting for him in the bark mulch. The unbearable images: Tess's bald head and eyelids and pubis, her small perfect lost left breast.

Breathe, breathe, he tells himself. He breathes through his mouth: The smell of the anaerobic compost makes him retch.

He hoses the barrel out, finds its lid, punches a couple of vents with a screwdriver, sets it up behind the garage. Surveys his morning's work: a good job.

And now to set out on his run, to shed this week, this year, of unhappiness.

He doesn't dare take his eyes off Sack, so has to inveigle him into the garage to look for the stroller, telling him that they're going to do something interesting. Sack whines that he wants to watch TV. The garage is full of junk – discarded IKEA furniture, mostly, as Lewis and Alison are buying real, hand-milled wood things now – and discarded appliances, replaced, still in good working order, by flashier models. Matt roots past cabinets, a washing machine and dryer. Enough stuff here to start two or three couples off in their first apartments. A project for him, probably – to get this all cleared out.

There's the navy nylon canvas of the jogging stroller, just where he'd remembered seeing it. He has to shift a sofa stacked with dining room chairs and lamps to get at it, but there it is. Bingo.

Our getaway vehicle, he says to Sack.

It's broken, Sack says.

Indeed, it is. One of its back wheels has been snapped cleanly off, right through the axle. It's still lying there, covered with oily garage-type dust.

So. That is that.

Sack hollers in protest: I want that! when Matt throws the stroller back into the corner, so Matt pulls it out, broken wheel as well, and drags it into the yard for Sack to play with. Unbearable to be inside on such a day. Sack pushes the broken stroller around the yard, ramming the azaleas.

Ah, Buddy. Don't do that.

Why not? Sack says. His grin is nihilist.

Hey, why not? Matt says. A few broken shrubs. Who will notice? And Sack will tire of it soon.

The afternoon trickles by. It is agonizingly slow. The day is beautiful, the first really warm day of April. The hills seem to pulse with freshness, just out of reach.

He digs through Sack's toys, piles an armload of stuff in a plastic tub, lugs it and the protesting Sack back outside. Locks the doors. Sack hollers and hollers, but when Matt dumps the contents of tub onto the lawn, squats down to look.

Matt picks up a remote control replica, the exact model and colour of the car he'd bought himself, a congratulatory prize, just before getting canned from his job. He and Tess had given the toy version to Sack for Christmas, the year before this. The wires have been pulled off, as well as one of the wheels.

I had this car, he says to Sack. Do you remember? I liked this car too much.

Sack grunts.

A strange fluke, that Tess and Alison had both got breast cancer. Not even the same kind of breast cancer. Not a genetic connection: They'd had the test. Just randomness. Just chance. Alison first, a few years ago. And then it had come back. Alison has maybe six months left; he's looked it up.

But Tess will get better. Is better.

He'd known Alison first – had known her before she and Lewis had gotten serious, when Lewis was still trying out a lot of different women, trading up, maybe. Sometimes he, Matt, the lesser-achieving sidekick, had dated the ones Lewis discarded. He'd been interested in Alison, had waited for her to turn to him in pique when someone else caught Lewis's eye. But Lewis had decided to park himself there. Maybe Matt had been too obvious in his appreciation, had made Lewis notice Alison's qualities.

Alison and Tess are small, dark-haired, quietly expressive women. Second generation Greek-Canadian. Tess is the older by two years. He'd met her at Lewis's and Alison's wedding; they'd been paired as attendants. That had been that. Tess had been like Alison only more so, the cool sinuousness, like something sleek moving in dappled shade.

You can't see anything of them in Sack, who is not in any way an endearing child. Sack is all Lewis, though Lewis has better table manners. But Lewis has no time for Sack.

Matt releases the next toy he has snatched up out of the tub: a half-sized bat and ball. He sees that they don't work together. The bat is actually meant to be used with an electronic game. It's weighted, but only plastic; it's meant to be swung at a virtual ball. The ball Matt has is from a different game. Matt can hear a rattling inside the bat.

You can't play with that, Sack says. It's broken.

Matt laughs.

That so, he says. He tosses the ball up, smacks it with the bat, which makes an ominous *ting* but remains intact. The ball arcs a little way and falls. Sack retrieves it, shrieking, and grabs at the bat. Matt lifts the bat out of his reach and sends the ball into the side of the garage, *smack*.

Let me, Sack says.

He connects with the ball on Matt's first toss, sends it up bouncing off the roof of the shed. The bat makes an electronic distress squeak. Sack laughs.

It's probably the first natural laugh Matt has heard from him in the whole six months he's been living here.

Those first two years when he had been working at getting Tess to fall in love with him, he and Tess and Lewis and Alison had been coagulating into two couples, into adults. The sharing of meals, of belongings, of camping trips. Sack had been born and Tess had held him, fresh from Alison's body, and looked at him in a way that told him it was time to press his luck, and he had, and they'd got married, in a ceremony calculated to complement but not rival or undermine Alison's and Lewis's. He had absolutely understood this, but it had been beautiful in spite of, or maybe because of, those constraints, the way he's always heard things can be.

In the tub are splintered building blocks and wheel-less toy cars; electronic learning games in cracked plastic housings with shredded paper decals; gnawed detailed plastic figurines of wild creatures; finely-sewed, glass-eyed puppets with limbs and hair ripped off. All the delicate and expensive toys Sack has been given, thoughtlessly, or maybe just too soon. Tess has talked about cleaning out his room, which overflows with junk, just so he can find the toys that still actually work, but Sack had set to howling, had thrown such a tantrum, when she'd suggested it.

They'll have a demolition party, a two-man derby, he and Sack. The smashing, the grinding, the crushing. It will make a good afternoon. He gets a fist-sized river rock from the driveway's edge, hunkers down beside Sack on the sidewalk, and mimes smashing the rock down on the replica car. He looks Sack in the eye, hands him the rock. Go on, Buddy, he says. Be my guest.

He's right. Sack enjoys this new game wholly. His cheeks flush pink, his greenish blond hair darkens with sweat, his lower lip, which tends to hang open, closes up over his piranha-like lower jaw. He sorts things thoughtfully, almost tenderly selecting what he wishes to destroy. He squats beside the driveway to select a better rock, one that fits his fist more comfortably and has a flattened snubbed business end. He pulverizes a small mountain of his damaged possessions, blocks and cars, miniature electronics, small porcelain heads and limbs, leaning into it, finding the toy's sweet spots, making of the crushing and grinding and splintering an art.

The afternoon passes. The others will be home soon. Lewis or Alison and Tess will be back to take over, Matt realizes. There might still be time for a run. Anyway, he'll be free: free to talk to Tess, to open his laptop, to do any number of things. That's not to be underestimated.

The sidewalk is littered with fragments of toys, with a flotsam of crushed plastic and metallic paint dust. He'll have to sweep it up. In his mind's eye, Matt sees the dark stain behind the shed where he dumped the rain barrel. Shit. That too.

But no: A few days in the air will take care of that anaerobic bacterial odour. Wholesome decomposition will ensue. The gloves, he'll bury.

He stands up, stretches, straightens his back. Don't let the bastards grind you down, he says to Sack.

Bastards, Sack says, thoughtfully.

That's right, Sack, he says.

He'll take the boy out here, next weekend, take Sack's clean shining unused real stainless steel miniature gardening tool set, and let the child loose. Out of a half-acre spread of lawn, Lewis can spare a little digging space. Sack can pit his unholy energy against the topsoil.

Matt will watch a video. He'll learn how to break up turf with a spade. He'll set Sack loose against the earth itself. Something interesting might happen. Something will be experienced first-hand. Something will respond the way it's supposed to. Something will be appeased.

THE CANOE

THEY ARE CANOEING THIS YEAR near Blue River, in mountains that are not quite far enough east to be the Rockies, but are, Kirsten says, rocky enough. She is brittle today, full of what Evan calls *smart remarks*, but what she sees as sticky patches, adhesive bandages, placed all over herself where there are cracks. There has been an argument in the car. She feels battered, as if they've been in a minor accident, and is already composing in her head the amusing and only slightly bitter account of the dispute that she'll tell to Linda later, perhaps when they've gone off into the underbrush to pee. The putting-together of this account calms her, like the rolling of string into balls. Only her surface, her top layer, remains delicate, and she must patch and fill fast enough that it doesn't disintegrate entirely.

Meanwhile there's the business of getting the canoes off the cars and onto the convenient trolleys the park provides and piling the tents and sleeping bags and air mattresses and coolers into them. It's a routine, like surgery: They have their moves down pat. Evan and Jeff sling the Bean's red canoe from the top of their SUV, while Kirsten and Linda steady the first trolley. Then they brace the other trolley while the green canoe is lifted from Evan and Kirsten's wagon, and settled with a gentle thump. Jeff has already opened the hatch of his vehicle and is tossing out the bright cylindrical packages. Evan does the same with theirs. Kirsten and Linda catch. Kirsten drops. They are slippery, these nylon capsules. A clatter as she fumbles, tent poles inside jostling, fibreglass on fibreglass. Watch it! Evan snaps, pausing in his throw. Whoops, she's broken the pattern. But Jeff flashes her a grin, a wink, out of Evan's line of sight. A consolation prize. She smiles weakly, grateful and embarrassed at the same time, as if, naked, she's been thrown a towel.

Then the coolers are lifted, placed in the bottoms of the canoes. Their cooler is heavy, packed with meals that she has cooked and frozen and wrapped individually, in foil and then slide-seal bags. They'll eat their way to the centre, as things thaw. (Well, not really. They'll eat their way downwards, through bricks of chili and butter chicken, beef ragout, pesto sauce and pasta, fat pork sausages.) Everything frozen solid, packed in ice. Linda and Jeff's cooler, she knows, contains something similar. They have been doing these trips for many years. They have it down to an art.

Paddles in, last, and then the cars locked, re-checked: beeps and flashes. Evan pulls wire mesh from a disjointed heap at the end of the parking lot, kicks a chunky roll towards Jeff, and they wrap the vehicles' wheels, unspooling the mesh around the base of the vehicles as if winding ribbon around hats, or cakes. Something bridal. It's for the porcupines, who like to gnaw tire rubber, god knows why, for they could hardly have evolved to eat rubber. Linda says she thinks they are attracted to the salt, the winter road salt that has permeated the rubber, that is imbedded in the treads. Kirsten says she suspects the porcupines are a myth, anyway. Evan and Jeff just like to tie things up. Linda laughs.

Or maybe, Kirsten says, they chew rubber for boredom. *Out of.* She means out of boredom. When she's had one of her pills she mixes her prepositions up: a very specific kind of brain zap that she suspects is psychosomatic. (Prepositions: the words that tell us the relationships of things in time and space. It's the definition she gives her students.) Perhaps the pills get between the synapses that understand time and space and short-circuit them. Or is it a language problem? Either way, a minor side effect. The pills work.

Maybe, Kirsten says, the porcupines chew the rubber tires out of boredom.

Drop it, Evan says, menacing.

On the trail, Jeff and Evan push the trolleys with the laden canoes, while Linda and Kirsten guide the bows. Even in June, at this altitude, the ground is just thawed, and boggy in patches, and the clay portage path treacherous under-foot. Kirsten and Linda are supposed to watch for exposed roots, rocks that might catch the trolleys' wheels and tip them. They are supposed to call out warnings. Linda is better at this. Kirsten forgets to pay attention to the ground in front of her. Evan sighs when the wheels of his trolley catch.

The trail is beautiful, winding through darkness and light: dense dark spruce and more open fir. *Gymnosperm*, Kirsten thinks. Naked seed. Linda taught her this term. She thinks of Greco-Roman wrestling, though: lithe, impossibly sinewy bodies tumbling in graceful arcs.

Linda has told her that the hard, resinous needles of conifers conserve moisture, an advantage in cold dry climates. The trees seem alive, Kirsten had said, then.

They are alive, Linda had corrected her, puzzled. But what she had meant was, they seem human.

Along the edge of the path grow mosses, the paired pink bells of the twinberry, the white solitary dogtooth violet in its serene quartet of leaves. The low yank-yank of a nuthatch, the gin scent of the creeping juniper. Kirsten feels herself open to the pleasure of the scent, the wood, its many small voices. Even the pores of her skin are ears. How lucky to have this. To have the canoe, and Jeff and Evan, who insist on this ritual trip, and Linda, who after all these years, still doesn't get her, but has taught her the magical names of the birds and the wildflowers. Tears blur her eyes.

How's the migraine? Linda asks, and Kirsten says, Oh, gone, mostly.

Those new pills really work, huh, Linda says. She knows Kirsten's migraines, which have dogged every trip for years.

They'd better, Kirsten says, at fifteen bucks a shot.

Good thing you have extended medical, Linda says.

Kirsten thinks about not being able to afford the pills, and shuts her eyes for a second.

And no side effects, huh, Linda says.

No side effects, Kirsten says firmly. She doesn't see explaining the space/time thing.

Behind them Jeff and Evan push the trolleys, as if wheeling gurneys. They appear similar, Kirsten thinks, like models chosen to set each other off, but not by too much, in a magazine ad. Evan is a little greyer; Jeff's hair is curly. But they wear similar bland middle-aged professional faces, similar khaki-coloured windbreakers, striped golf shirts, dark chino shorts. Both the same medium-tall height, both with the build that comes from twice weekly runs, occasional squash games: a build that is neither lean nor going to fat, but somewhere in-between. It's as if they had decided at some point in their lives to become twins, and have been quite successful at that undertaking.

Kirsten says to Linda, under cover of the noise of the trolleys, Evan is such a prick, we had such a stupid argument loading the car this morning. Can you believe it; he said we shouldn't have brought the cooler. He said we should travel lighter.

What did he think you'd eat? Linda says.

I don't know. Fish, maybe. A lot of fish.

Jeff's the same, Linda says, equably. He didn't want to bring the tent.

Oh god. Imagine the bugs, Kirsten says. (But imagines the stars, the kissing sounds of carp rising in the night lake.)

They are suddenly shouting to be heard, and Kirsten realizes that it is the chop of a helicopter, drowning their voices.

She hadn't recognized it at first, oddly. But there it is, right over them, and deafening, now.

They all four stop on the path, heads tilted back, staring up. (Like statues of awed yokels, Kirsten thinks.) The helicopter is green, official, with the maple leaf on the side and numerals, letters, on the underside. They can see two figures inside, both wearing headphones. It's not clear which is the pilot. Then the helicopter swings back out over the lake and is gone.

My god, what was that about? Kirsten asks.

And Jeff says that it's likely search and rescue, that when he went into the parks building to buy their passes and pick up the trolleys, one of the rangers had told him that a couple of canoeists had been lost, last seen just above the falls.

Evan whistles, a low, long intake of breath, and Linda exclaims that it's terrible, but Kirsten falls silent, because she suddenly sees what she has known all along: The crack has been widening all day, and somebody has fallen in, more than one person, and it is reaching now to her very feet. And she is unable to move, they've gone on without her. But then Evan is at her ear, near, beside, *inside* her ear, muttering at her to *just behave*, and she covers her ears with her hands and strides off down the trail.

And then the lake, held like a sleeping mirror by the blue peaks.

AT ITS MOUTH THE LAKE IS MARSHY, and the water, between the clumps of cattails and floating islands of lilies, is sombre jade. Kirsten lies back in the bow, trailing her hand in the warmer upper inches of the water, parting the duckweed.

The water pushing against the canoe is thick with suspended particles, green corpuscles. Underneath, carp are gliding along arched passageways, mouthing the liquid world. The water plants twining, voluptuous tunnels.

Evan fishes from the canoe, casting out his line, reeling it in, casting out and reeling in. The whir and click of the reel, the quick flight and gradual closing in of the tackle, are hypnotic. And in Evan's even casts, a profound satisfaction, an entrenched contentment, that is actually relaxing.

Evan had spent all winter refurbishing the canoe, stretching its new fibreglass skin over the wooden ribs, scraping and moulding, heating glue, coaxing and cobbling the vessel back into working order. He is good with his hands, a surgeon. He liked her to be his helper, hand him things. Sometimes she did, if she weren't too busy, if she'd had a glass of wine or two, in the evening, and was feeling peaceable, detached.

She had argued for replacing the canoe with two light new kayaks, ones they could have carried separately. Had imagined herself taking the kayak down to the river, in the winter, when the swans patrolled its banks, slipping silently among them. She'd even suggested to the girls that they could contribute to the kayaks, make them a joint Christmas present. *What can I get you and Dad?* they always moan, in November. *You're so hard to buy for.* But the girls had both argued against the idea, vehemently. They loved the old canoe's shape, its idiosyncrasies. You couldn't buy a canoe like that, now. It had character. Though they are both living on their own now, one in university, one working, they are still heavily invested in the securities of their childhood, she understands. They need the canoe: For them, it is still cradle, or womb. She understands this, understands their need to have still, beneath them, stable ground. A childhood of happy canoe trips and placid, nurturing parents paddling in unison.

The helicopter can be heard, then seen, miles down the lake, tracking up the shoreline.

Still haven't found them, Evan says. Kirsten remembers the lost canoeists, the conversation the day before.

Strange to think they're probably in the lake, she says.

Yes, Evan says. At the bottom, by now.

The lake is immensely deep, with steep sides for most of its perimeter. It doesn't turn over. The bottom is a place of mystery, dark and unreachable, like space.

They won't be found, then, Kirsten says.

I don't know, Evan says. They will float up, I think. He is dispassionate; he is familiar with bodies.

When? Kirsten asks.

Evan shakes his head.

Maybe, Kirsten says, they won't sink. They'll be carried along, just under the surface. Where would they end up, then?

Here, Evan says, after a pause. Here, near the marsh. Where the lake exits. The currents all head here.

Kirsten looks around. Away from the marsh, where there is open water, the surface is blue, opaque, hard and glittery as mica. The lake appears slippery rather than liquid, dazzling, impermeable, a metallic tissue. Ahead, a pair of grebes, startled, runs across the surface and flaps off toward the trees.

She had not thought, last fall, that she would agree to the canoeing trip this year. Had thought: the girls are gone. There is nothing to confine us.

The world is watery, deceptive, impenetrable.

LATE JUNE IS THE WRONG TIME TO CAMP, this far north. It's far too bright, the nights are too short, this close to the solstice. At 11 it's still light enough in the tent for Kirsten to see Evan's slightly averted profile, his high brow and nose and full lips. Evan has fallen asleep, as always, instantaneously, as if he's been clubbed over the head. There are no layers, for him, between consciousness and unconsciousness: just a simple switch. On/off. For her, though, sleep is a location to which she must drift down slowly. As she falls, fronds of the day's thoughts, sensations, brush her again. She is aware of this vegetation becoming gradually more elaborate, more unlikely, more irresistible. And the slightest noise or movement will jerk her back to the surface. She must always fall asleep after Evan does, and her slow drifting often takes hours.

The morning journey, though, happens in reverse. She passes from sleep, even from deep dreaming sleep, effortlessly and instantly, as if stepping through a doorway. Evan wakes laboriously, groans, thrashes, yawns profoundly, as though he is being dragged back against his will, extradited into consciousness. His loud yawns, his leg jerks usually wake Kirsten long before she's had her fill of rest. Wake her to a sense of disappointment, grievance.

It's no use. Sleep is unattainable, tonight. There is no preliminary softening of edges, only the inadequate depth of the air mattress. Kirsten rises, unzips the tent's door and slips out into the oily light.

Jeff is on the shore, gazing out toward the lake. On the sand beside him, a lantern, not lit, and a paperback copy of poems by Jack Gilbert. Without looking up, he moves the lantern, the book, and she sits. Jeff's hand moves discreetly and brings up a small object, finger-shaped, that glimmers a faint white. He proffers it to Kirsten in his upturned palm. It takes her a moment to recognize it.

Oh – yes, please.

He puts it in his own mouth, lights it with a long barbecue lighter, and draws on it quickly, a series of staccato puffs, until the end glows, and then passes it to Kirsten.

Too light for camping, this time of year, he says.

Yes. Solstice.

But quiet, at least.

Yes. She says. Evan can sleep anytime, though.

Linda wears a blindfold.

Evan will be up at four.

Hopefully not chopping wood?

Such complicity, and all done with inflection, so subtly, that to try to put a finger on it, to say *there, there*, would be to extinguish it.

The lake gleams briefly, here and there, as the dusk thickens, condenses. Loons call, their voices juddering over the surface like skipped stones. Kirsten and Jeff pass the joint between them. It's as if they're taking turns blowing up a balloon. Their fingers brush.

Jeff reaches for the folded blanket that lies next to him and throws it around both of them, slipping his arm around her shoulders to do so. She can feel each woollen fibre of each strand of the blanket's fringe as it trails across her bare right arm. Her left arm brushes his right, the hairs on his forearm touch her individually. But the touch is not intrusive; it is a delicate inscribing of boundary. It outlines her, both of them, defines where they begin and leave off. It is utter separateness, utter safety.

SHE DREAMS A JERKY, disjointed dream. She is walking along her cul-de-sac, at home, in a filmy aqua nightgown, like a 60s film star, Anne Bancroft, might have worn. In her dream she faints. The street becomes water, thick and beating with micro-organisms, pulsing around her. Then Linda is also there. She and Jeff and Evan lift Kirsten into the canoe and hoist her onto their shoulders.

Now they carry her through the forest, through the stately, overarching fir and spruce, the dappled shade. She feels guilty, fraudulent. But she lets them carry her.

A rhythm of footsteps grows louder, and she realizes they are walking amid a crowd. Through the ribs and skin of the canoe, the fibreglass cloth that is patched, even transparent, in places, she can see a multitude of men and women, in suits, in legal robes, surgical scrubs. She can't make out their faces, but she knows them. They are marching in a group, and she is being carried in the centre of it, trapped in her diaphanous gown.

When she wakes, the beating of feet has become a helicopter's chop. Later, when they return to the park entrance, they'll hear that the bodies were found that morning.

THE TROUT TASTES OF MUD: it is too late in the year, already.

Evan and Jeff announce that they will go help search for the missing couple. They have canoed in this lake for years, since they were boys. They know its currents and rhythms, they say. They have an idea. (They have no idea.)

While they're gone, Kirsten and Linda hike along the shore; they are looking for a path up to an alpine meadow that they think they remember, from an earlier trip. The beach trail curves through a marshy area, a giants' wood box of standing dead spruce and tumbled, blackened logs. Where wood is exposed, it is ashy.

Fire, Kirsten says.

No – flood, Linda says. The spruce choked with sudden, sporadic engorgements of the lake, in past years, high-water years. The black, the ash, a mineral crust, from leached salts.

They find a trail that ascends through the spruce, a dim cleft stitched loosely together with spiders' webs. Farther on, though, where it cuts across an open slope, the trail is blocked by a recent fall of shale.

What the hell, Linda says, surprisingly.

They could go around, through the scrub and spruce, but decide to scramble up. There's a trick to it, Kirsten finds. If you try to track up horizontally, the shale starts slipping and you're soon fighting an avalanche of rocks and dust. You have to take a run at it, instead, go diagonal, spraddle-legged, grasping whatever tussocks of plant you can. And you can't follow anyone else up. You have to make your own path, or you collide with all of the debris in your partner's wake.

She and Linda begin the ascent, taking parallel routes, but

suddenly, she is in difficulty. Her legs won't move fast enough, and she is sliding, the shale carrying her downwards, though she is still climbing.

Help! she calls, half-joking, and Linda calls back, *Run!* But the rocks above her begin to cascade down, their flinty edges striking her shins. She stops.

I'll go the long way round, she calls up.

But Linda slides down, grabs her hand, and pulls her, at a run, back up the slope. And after a moment she gets her wind back, is able to scramble faster and faster, till they both collapse, laughing and winded, where the path resumes.

In the meadow, an *embarras de richesses*. Linda names the flowers: Marguerites, monkshood, Indian paintbrush.

Arnica, fireweed, gentian.

Harebell, lupine, snow lily.

They find a sun-warmed boulder, an occasional, dropped by a glacier, and sip from their water bottles. Linda lies back against the dark rock, shaking out her light hair.

Ticks, Kirsten reminds.

Oh, who gives a damn, Linda says. She stretches her legs, tugs up the elastic cuffs of her wind pants, so that her strong tan shins shine in the sun. Biologist, marathoner, mother of sons: Linda, in Kirsten's inner eye, is always running with whistle and ball in a scrum of small boys. Sturdy, matter-of-fact. Her flesh and bone a cage, a barrier against the merely imaginative. But now, sprawled back on the rock, she seems aqueous, of another element.

Linda turns her head, looks at Kirsten sideways under lowered lids.

Jeff doesn't care for flowers, you know, Linda says. He's colour-blind. Also, he doesn't have a very good sense of smell.

Oh, the layers in her voice. The currents, the swirl of sediment.

THE LAKE WATER IS COLD, beyond cold. It is compressing her chest, her blood vessels, even though the initial shock of it, the burn on her skin, has numbed. The lake was likely frozen over until only a few weeks ago.

Kirsten pictures the breaking up of the ice, to keep her mind from the growing ache in her fingers and toes: the infra-sonic booms as it began to fissure, the dreaming world below beginning to stir. Fish and amphibians, molluscs, aquatic insects, safely tucked in their mud beds, wrapped in their own antifreeze, but stupefied with cold, with lack of oxygen, slowly coming to consciousness. What has she read in a jour-nal, lately: that hibernating squirrels wake with pounding headaches, from the shutdown of their systems, the buildup of toxins. Perhaps fish and frogs do as well.

She hears her name shouted across the water, turns from her slow crawl to see Evan, who has woken and is standing on the shore, very far away. From here the tents look like toys, like the models in camping-goods stores. Now, Linda and Jeff emerge from their tent, half-dressed, stand in an odd posture, something between controlled concern and panic.

Kirsten! Evan booms. Come back, now!

She lifts an arm to wave, and resumes her swimming. She is not spent, not frozen, yet. In fact, she is somewhat warmer: Her body is starting to immure itself; she is finding her stroke. She is a strong swimmer.

Evan shouts again, real fear in his voice. (His fear a bottom-dwelling creature, with atrophied eyes, mouth feelers.)

She can no longer make out their words, but can hear the voices of the others, on the shore, calling to each other about blankets, life jackets, no doubt. They sound delighted that something is happening. She hears the scrape of the canoe being launched: not the Beans' lighter, newer one, but their old heavy craft.

Evan had bought that canoe soon after they were married, bought it second-hand, from a neighbour. It had been the first important thing they'd bought.

He'd been the first of whom she had thought: *He will do.*

She can hear the fast slap of the paddles, now, getting closer.

On the brink, she had known: We have little in common. We do not think on the same plane. But had said to herself: The more you have in common, the finer and finer hairs you will split between you. Taxonomy is in our nature.

She slows her strokes. It is almost time to turn around now. She isn't tired; instead, she feels hyper-alert, as if the immersion has woken her up, not from hibernation, but from something like it. She glances over her shoulder: Evan is paddling, Jeff crouched in the bows. Jeff calls something to her that she doesn't understand: There is water in her ears. She hears, though, a kind of scorn, a kind of thin twitch at the underskin that is different from Evan's blunt hungry strike, but not altogether different.

The canoe is almost on her. Ah, fuck, she thinks. There will be no escape.

But she turns around, treading water briefly, and begins to swim back towards the shore.

CLEARWATER

IN THE MORNING Bryan follows the North Thompson, which is grey, sluggishly rippled, like a black-and-white photo of water, north and east, towards the mountains, toward the headwaters. The highway hugs the mountainsides, is flung back and forth in wide loops, rising from the floodplain to precarious slopes.

He had telephoned Roy Tuesday night, long enough ahead that Roy won't feel rushed, close enough to the visit that he won't forget. But he still doesn't know how he'll find the old guy. It's not as if Roy goes anywhere, or takes the trouble to clean up the place more than usual, or fixes a meal when he comes. More that he needs the time to get himself organized mentally, for the visit. Bryan can understand that. You get pulled along by the current of your life, and it takes a little time and effort to swing out into another routine. He guesses it will be like that for him, too, when he's Roy's age.

Rayleigh, Vinsulla, McLure, Louis Creek: the little towns along the highway. Grassland on either side of the road and the river. The grass bleached out by the summer's heat, dotted by sagebrush, that purple-green colour he can't name. And then crumbling grey and yellow rock, the highway now cut off from the river by cliffs, and the black stubble of trees on both sides, where the fire leapt the canyon. An uncompromising landscape. Sere. He has driven it too many times to count, but it always impresses him, the harshness, how the trees and grass can survive on so little.

The first time must have been that summer he was eight. The two of them, Bryan and Jenny, driving up from Vancouver on the Trans-Canada, then the Yellowhead, the landscape, after the mountains, getting browner by the mile, and Bryan changing to a new radio station when the one from the last town got too fuzzy. Then they were past Kamloops, where they'd stopped at the Dairy Queen and both had small cones, and Bryan had found a quarter under the floor mat so he'd been allowed to have his cone dipped.

Cowboy country, Jenny had said. Yellowhead Highway; I love it. Then later: This landscape is awesome! Like a road-runner cartoon. And later still: I'm sick of this. Looks like someone forgot to water the grass.

That must have been around Barrière. They were headed for Jasper, but it was almost night, so they would have to sleep in a campground. That's how they'd ended up in Clearwater, at Roy's.

Here he is at Barrière now. Another bridge, this one punched-out steel, with rivets and cables showing, so you could see how it was put together. Not reassuring. Like that stuff boys used to have, the metal stuff. Meccano. Did kids still play with it?

Birch Island, Darfield, Little Fort, Blackpool. Old railway stops, not even whistle-stops now, some of them: just names. He likes that the signs are still there. He likes to know where he's going. He likes to know where he is. The landscape lusher, here: green fields, dense trees in the deep shadows of the hills. Autumn colours and a pheasant scudding across a frosted pasture. The dull flicker under his collarbone: remembering his dream years ago of buying some property, living here, and then the realization he wouldn't, ever.

And then the town, just past where the Clearwater River flows into the North Thompson, and the turnoff, and the short road through the trees.

WAITING WHILE ROY stumps across the house to the door, Bryan casts his gaze to the porch roof, runs the edge of his thumbnail along a suspicious joist. He'd noticed the slope of the roof as he walked up to the house. Sagging at the left outside corner. Not his business: Roy's still perfectly capable of getting someone to take care of it. But a shame to let things fall apart. The timber gives spongily under his nail, as he expected. He drops his arm, turns around just in time for the door to open, timing it by Roy's approaching steps.

And there's Roy, all jut of grey beard and belly, low-slung jeans, high-tension suspenders, wheezing a little and frowning, as if Bryan were a Bible salesman, as if he's never seen him before. But at the sight of Roy, at the rush of warm, coffee-and-dog-pee (though the dog isn't here anymore, died a couple of years ago) scented air that puffs out around Roy, Bryan feels the breath return to his body, feels his shoulders relax.

They're not the sort to hug, either of them. Bryan holds out the case he's brought, beer in bottles, and Roy grunts and gestures to come inside, and stumps back through the kitchen, Bryan following, looking around, as always, at the pinky-beige lino, the speckled countertops and newer white appliances, and seeing under them, as always, the worn aqua-blue tiles, the Harvest Gold fridge and range, the metal-edged laminate, of his childhood occupancy. In the living room, Bryan's eyes go to the photos ranged along the shelves; there is the familiar parade of Roy's two kids through the seventies, photos faded so both of them have pastel clothes and soft brown hair, as if they're preserved in soft-focus. Then more recent photos of kids of various sizes: Roy's grandkids, babies and toddlers in Christmas outfits, and Bryan's two boys.

No pictures of Jenny or of Roy's previous wife. No photos of Bryan growing up.

He's learned already that there isn't a sign of himself in the house. Why would there be?

The room he'd had at Roy's is still there, of course. The first time he'd brought Lori, he'd asked to see it. It hadn't been the same: It had been painted, had different furniture. The ceiling had been too low, the window too small. It had not seemed familiar at all. Then he'd asked about his things, the racing cars, the sled. Roy had said, feel free to look around. He had. They weren't there.

WHAT'S NEW IN YOUR NECK of the woods? Bryan hears himself say, then winces – he sounds like an old man, older than Roy.

Roy ignores the question, though. He picks up a folded newspaper, holds it out toward Bryan, shaking it up and down as if to settle the words.

You see this? Roy asks.

Bryan takes the paper, knowing what he'll see, approximately. Something about Iraq. His eyes scan the half-sheet. No, it's Canada. The environment. He scans the article, composes a non-committal reply. The thing about Roy, he's not like the old people in Bryan's neighbourhood who can be counted on to have conservative views.

They never learn, Bryan says, which is a useful response at any time. Bryan isn't so keen on arguing politics with Roy. Roy knows too much, makes him feel like a fool, whatever Bryan says. He hands the paper back to Roy, still folded. Roy grunts again, almost a disappointed sound, and lays the paper back on the couch.

You keeping well? Bryan asks.

Roy nods gravely; says, Can't complain. He says it with the same dignity with which he took his seat: a sort of gracious acceptance of the world's shortcomings.

They sit for a while.

You want some coffee? Roy asks. I got some fresh in the pot, if you want to get it. Some baking from the store across the highway, too.

Bryan wanders into the kitchen. You got a new coffee maker, Bryan calls.

Yeah, Roy says. Darn thing turns itself on in the morning. Fresh coffee before you even know it.

Roy is taking care of himself still, Bryan thinks. The kitchen looks scrubbed. Clean bag in the trash can. Good that Roy's looking after things. He feels he should offer to fix something, but he can't see anything that he could do quickly. When he comes back to the living room, Roy puts down the paper again.

This Harper guy, he says. Afraid to stand up to Big Brother. We should be ashamed, as Canadians. It wasn't always like that.

No, sir, Bryan says. He remembers that Roy is actually American, one of the original draft dodgers. Though that's all over with. What's the word. *Amnesty.* And that American politician, what was his name, meeting them all in Nelson a couple of years ago, dedicating the monument. Well, times change. When he and Jenny had met Roy, though, there'd been some question of Roy's legal status. Some possibility of his still being extradited, or deported, or whatever it was. Which made Roy's choice of profession kind of interesting, if you thought about it.

Roy looks like he wants to show Bryan something in the newspaper, but then folds the paper up again, drops it and sighs.

How're the boys doing? he asks.

Oh, fine, Bryan says. He curls his hands around the mug, stands closer to the wood stove. He used to bring his kids up to see Roy, a couple of times a year, when they were younger. When a car outing was something they jumped at. Lori too.

Lori always made sure they visited Roy, always sent him a card at Christmas and went to the trouble of packing up a box of baking and some gift, those gloves with the removable mitten top or something like that, things that women think a man wants. Bryan used to be pleased by this effort, though; he should remember that. There was a time when he would have said, *Lori has a soft spot for Roy*, or, *Roy has a soft spot for Lori*, though he has come to realize that isn't likely true, only a way he liked to see it.

Now Lori can't be bothered with sending things up for Roy. This is a means of punishing not Roy, but himself, he understands.

He skirts the topic of Lori, and gives his news of the boys. Jared's in high school now, he says. He tried out for basketball, but I think he's too short. Didn't make the team. He does okay in his classes, though. Gets Bs if he puts a little effort into it. Ty is another story; he can't be bothered. Could get As, could be a decent hockey player. If he'd of stuck to it, he could be playing rep, even at his age.

I suppose the boys are both engrossed in video games, Roy says, and Bryan sighs. That's it; that's it exactly. Kids don't want to play outside anymore, don't want to make things. That's some of the argument with Lori: the growing piles of expensive devices and games; the hours the boys spend immobile in darkened rooms, their faces lit by screens. He's afraid suddenly that Roy is going to ask something personal about himself and Lori, but he doesn't.

Roy says, instead, Must be a lot of entertainment value in them.

Yes, there is, Bryan says. He does not want to talk about video games, but he does not want to talk about Lori, or work, either.

Roy is silent for a few moments, his head nodding a little. Parkinson's, Lori had said once, but Roy says it is not.

As if he's on the same wavelength, Roy asks, then, Lori still working? Still nursing?

She is. (This morning, him feigning sleep, even through the rocking motion that was her sitting on the end of the bed putting on her pantyhose, till she was gone, and then another fifteen minutes or so, waiting for the house to heat to something closer to the bird's-nest temperature under the duvet. You need to get the boys up, she had said, clipped, before going out the door. As if he didn't, every morning.)

Roy nods and nods. Bryan has already told him, on his last visit, six months ago, about being laid off, and he doesn't ask if Bryan is back at work.

Economy's still slow, Roy says, though, and Bryan thinks it's a nod at his unemployed status.

Yes, sir, he says.

He works – or worked – for a company that sells heavy-duty equipment for mining.

Roy neither commiserates nor makes suggestions about how to get back on his feet, as his in-laws put it. Bryan feels a curious vertigo, as if he has braced for an impact that has not arrived.

How about some lunch? Roy says, finally.

It's only eleven, but Bryan jumps up as if reprieved.

There are sandwich fixings in the refrigerator, meats and cheese wrapped in butcher paper, and fresh, unsliced bakery bread, and soup that Bryan heats up in a saucepan. They sit at the table, Roy lowering himself into his chair with a kind of dignified heaviness. He slices the bread, makes Bryan's sandwich, asking him what he wants: Butter? Mayonnaise? Salt and pepper? The soup tastes homemade. Beef, barley, vegetables.

Bryan finishes too quickly. You went to town on that, Roy comments.

Roy is eating his own sandwich slowly, sipping his soup slowly, still with that dignity. He always had that, Bryan thinks. That slowness, that deliberateness. As if he were a rock. That's how he'd seen Roy, when he was a kid. Solid, fixed. Jenny, erratic as water.

He had come to like being in Roy's house, living with Roy. He had held Roy's hand whenever there had been the opportunity, though Roy hadn't encouraged this, only tolerated it, surely. He'd referred to Roy as his dad at school, as often as he could. For that part-year.

He looks around the kitchen: an old-fashioned one, with a formica table. White-painted cabinets. They'd been varnished wood, before. Jenny had painted on them: a flock of birds, yellow and green, winging across the maple, their bills open, their eyes bright. At the lower edge, she'd put in the mountains, with their rich dark spruce. Roy, he remembers, had said: You've got the scale wrong. Those birds would be two hundred feet across.

The birds are bigger because they're more important, Jenny had said.

The ghost of the painting must be still there, on the wood. He brushes a fingertip along the white paint, but there is no sign, no disruption in the flat white surface. Sanded down, first, likely. But under the white enamel, would the colours still exist, staining the wood?

HE REMEMBERS AGAIN, with that dull knock of repetition, his losses: the electric car set, the fancy racing sled. Like a needle stuck in a groove, he wants to ask Roy again if he can look in the basement, but they've already established, years ago, that none of Bryan's things have remained in Roy's house.

That year, that almost-year. Of course he remembers everything about his Christmas gifts. That had been his only family Christmas, his only real Christmas, maybe, until he and Lori had got married and made Christmas themselves, or more usually, gone to her family's. Of course he remembers everything about his gifts.

He and Jenny had left, had pulled out, before the next winter. The racing set had been left behind; he'd not had time to pack it. And the sled – that had been in the shed, and left behind too. Jenny had brought the tape deck Roy had given her, but her next boyfriend had stolen it, sold it to buy dope, likely.

He has never been able to call up the details of their exodus. Had it been day or night? Had they hitchhiked, that time, or caught the Greyhound? Had there been a sudden fight, had Roy kicked Jenny out? Or had they built a slow resentment, Jenny fuming silently, then making tracks while Roy was down at the station?

There's a leap to be made over something deep and cold and dangerous, and he can't trust that he won't fall in.

When they're finished eating, Bryan washes up the plates and bowls and cutlery, the saucepan, and stacks them in the drain rack, then joins Roy, who has headed back to his chair. Roy has not picked up the newspaper. He looks sleepy, now. Is he older than Bryan thinks?

SIT, ROY SAYS, but he can't sit. He never can sit still.

Roy never asks about Jenny. Bryan never mentions her, the way she lives, the stress of the continual crises.

The trip into Clearwater the first time, more than thirty years ago. Jenny driving that Celica, which was a kind of bronze-brown, a late model, and probably, Bryan thinks now, not actually Jenny's own car. He can't remember it much later than the trip, so possibly it was reclaimed by its real owner, who would have been Cliff, or perhaps Doug, who hadn't been Jenny's boyfriend, really, but a teenaged boy who she'd met at the midway, and brought home to the house she and Cliff had shared, which had resulted in her and Bryan leaving in some hurry.

The interior of the Celica had been cream. Leather seats. Himself curled up on the seat, next to Jenny. Trying not to drip ketchup or ice cream on the seat, not because Jenny was worried about it, but because he had naturally liked things to be neat and clean. He remembers the sky cut into blocks: cloud, blue, cloud. He had reclined the front passenger seat right back, and looked up through the sunroof, and Jenny was singing along to "The Gambler," making her voice deep like Kenny Rogers', and the sun blading through the blocks of cloud so that he was suffused with light, shadow, light.

He had seen, through the sunroof, a hawk, and had sat up quickly, scrabbling in his bag for his bird book and binoculars, which hadn't of course been there.

You should have remembered them, Jenny had said. But she'd pulled him out of his bed, into the car, when they had left Cliff's, so quickly that most of his stuff had been left behind.

Maybe Cliff will send my stuff, he'd said. But Jenny had made a face. I don't think so.

His lost sled, his car set. They have almost lost their shine, now; he's brought them up too often, used them to shame his sons, when they've left one of their perpetual messes of toys or games uncared for, unvalued. The impatience in Jared's voice, just this last week. We've heard the story a million times, Dad. Your deprived childhood.

YESTERDAY: HE HADN'T MEANT. Only Jared, so mouthy. So full of himself. Didn't mean to do that. But the kid pouring half a six-dollar box of cereal in the bowl, the bowl nearly overflowing, the kid slack-jawed, blank-eyed. The number of half-eaten bowls of cereal he's carried upstairs from the play-room. Oblivious.

Hey! Dad! That's my cereal!

Look. Just. Look how much.

I'm gonna eat it!

He hadn't meant to get into it, the tussle. The kid's fault, grabbing the box back. Insolent. He'd fought off every instinct to shake Jared's silly stubborn head off his shoulders.

Dad! Let go! I'm trying to get some breakfast! Do you want me to go to school or not?

The room suddenly crowding him into a small, powerless place.

Have it then!

His own face nose-to-nose with his son's. The momentary rush and release of letting go, letting his vocal cords expand fully, his clenched hands move, tipping the bowl of ash-brown flakes, of blue milk, over his son's head.

Lori: You have no idea how to be a father.

WHEN JARED WAS BORN, Lori's mom had come to look after Lori and the baby for the first week or so, and the three of them, Lori and her mom and the baby, had made this tight group, in which there really wasn't room for Bryan. Bryan had not thought: *I have a son*, but, *I wonder if Roy is still up there in Clearwater?* And he was. He'd gone straight to the library – no computer at home, then, not like now – and found the Clearwater directory and Roy still in it.

Bryan had driven up, by himself the first time, a few weeks after Jared was born. He hadn't been back, at that point, for sixteen years, but he'd found it easily enough, the cluster of diner and garage, tattoo shop at the turnoff, the bed-and-breakfasts with their signs in German, the small houses, many of them mobile homes with layers of porches and carports added on, as if trying to assume permanence, legitimacy.

He had found the street he had walked along, to and from school, that year, scuffing his winter boots through the snow, cracking the thin ice of the puddles underfoot in early spring.

The mailboxes, still in the same place. It had all seemed smaller and shabbier than he remembered, of course. But he'd been pleased at that, too.

He'd thought that Roy was happy to see him. He was never sure. Roy remembered him, but he didn't seem like he needed company all that much. Roy had another family: He'd had a marriage and kids before Bryan and Jenny came along. And he must have had women friends, even ones with kids, after Bryan and Jenny, though Bryan does not like to think of that. But he did not tell Bryan not to come.

A boy needs a dad, Jenny had said, because she had fallen in love with Roy's voice on the radio announcing "Rhinestone Cowboy." Roy ran a little independent radio station, in those days. He was a draft dodger, an American, and there still hadn't been amnesty, but Roy had been on that radio every day, talking to the people around Clearwater in his deep, slow voice intoning the names of songs, or maybe important information, like *I highly recommend the blueberry pie being served down at Charlene's today,* or *Would the owners of the chartreuse Pinto please move it as Chuck can't get his Jimmy out of his driveway.* Roy, dispensing moods as he saw fit, the slow songs like "Tequila Sunrise" and "Could I Have This Dance for the Rest of My Life"; the quicker ones like "Cinnamon Girl" and "Could Have Been a Lady" and "Your Backyard." Roy winding the day up and slowing it down. *Here's one for all of you folks out on the east cut.*

To hear Roy's steady baritone on the radio and think: That's my dad. He had worked at that; he had polished up that thought.

ROY LOOKS OUT OF THE picture window now, and Bryan, following his gaze, sees that it has started to snow, suddenly, very heavily, flakes of snow coming down big and flat as torn paper, wastebaskets of the stuff, lacing through the bare weak yellow branches of the willow. Big, wet flakes, gluing themselves to the ground, obliterating the lawn with a startling quickness. It snows so much more up here, up against the Rockies, than where he lives, and the snow is so much wetter, heavier.

It had been his first real snow, that winter he had lived in Clearwater – it hadn't snowed much in Vancouver. He and Jenny had played in it like kids, snowball fights, snow angels, snow men. Roy coming in, from shovelling the driveway, snow in his beard, watching them, smiling in his dignified way. Solid, apart.

What had it meant for Roy, having him and Jenny there? That's what he's always wanted to know. What had it meant?

He and Jenny had driven from the coast, where it was lush and rainy, through the very dry land, cowboy country, and then stopped at Clearwater, where it was rainy again and the forest dense with hemlock and cedar, thick green vines and bushes that he hadn't been there long enough to learn the names of. They had been on their way to Jasper, and had stopped on a whim, and then the next summer, before school was out, they'd left. They hadn't gone to Jasper, though – only back to Vancouver, to a lot of change, a lot of different addresses. He hadn't lived in one place for more than a few months until Jenny had got together with Don. Then a couple of years in one spot, in a decent house. But Bryan hadn't got along with Don, and had moved out pretty soon after that.

Roy says, You'll want to be hitting the road soon; it's really coming down.

Yes, and he hasn't put the snow tires on the pickup yet. He ought to be going. He'll go, in a minute.

But he sits down, finally takes his seat on the slip-covered sofa. You want any wood cut? he asks Roy. Groceries? He can stay and shovel the driveway, maybe, so Roy's caretaker can make her way in.

The snow is coming down as if it can't stop itself. He hasn't seen it snow anywhere else like it snows here, in these huge, heavy flakes, like the snow is being poured over the edge of something.

HE TURNS TO ROY, to say, Remember that Christmas, remember carrying me back from the toboggan hill, but Roy has fallen asleep, his eyes closed, his head held upright against the back of his chair, his big body perfectly immobile, as if he'd been rooted in one place for years and years.

THAT FIRST TRIP UP HERE, over thirty years ago now. Jenny driving the stolen Celica, the landscape becoming green as they neared the mountains, as they came close to Clearwater. Bryan had found a new station on the radio, and a man's deep voice was announcing a song, a country song, and Jenny had said, My God, I'm in love with that man! I'm going to stop here and find him!

And Bryan said No, no don't, Mom, but Jenny laughed. Why not? You could use a dad.

And he remembers that they drove right up to Roy's door,

and Jenny hopped out of the car, swinging her bag over her shoulder, and knocked on the door, and Roy came out onto the porch, looking surprised (you could see more of his mouth then; his beard wasn't so bushy) and Jenny said, hi, we've come to live with you. And Bryan had carried in his own bag, with his spare underwear and jeans and the jackknife that Cliff, Jenny's last boyfriend, had given him, the one thing he'd managed to keep, and walked into a room with a bed and dresser and a little table by the bed with a lamp on it, and put his underwear and jeans and T-shirts into the drawers.

Of course it couldn't have been like that. There must have been a space of time; there must have been a place they stayed while Jenny made inquiries and met Roy in a bar or something and fixed it up so he'd let them move in. He knows that. He remembers the campground; maybe they stayed there for a few days, or maybe there was a motel, or a room in someone else's house. Jenny was good at getting people to take them in, take care of them. They must have been in Clearwater some time before Jenny found Roy.

But Bryan can't remember that. He'd swear that they'd driven right up to Roy's house. He'd swear that Roy had opened that door, and said, well, hey, Bryan. There's lots of room for a boy, here. You just come right on in.

The snow falling steadily, the big wet flakes piling up. Roy asleep in his chair.

JENNY MUST HAVE BEEN WHAT, twenty-three, when they came to live with Roy. And Roy? He can't tell, doesn't know Roy's age now, even. Maybe he'd been in his forties then. To children, all adults look about the same age until they're old. He had thought Roy was old, though: much older than Jenny.

Bryan had been born when Jenny was fifteen. They'd been only fifteen years apart, he and Jenny. He thinks, now: She was the same age his son Jared is now when he was born. A child. Fifteen.

Jenny had never had other children, though she'd tried, he thinks: when he was in his teens, when she'd married Don, when she'd been sober for a while. Lori said once that likely his birth was really hard on Jenny's body; she hadn't been mature enough, and had been damaged somehow. Lori knew that kind of thing; she was a nurse. Though it pissed him off, when she said things about Jenny. Jenny was a mess, sure. It was bad. But Lori didn't know everything. She didn't know.

It had been just the two of them. Like two kids together.

At first the snow seems to have let up a little, but then the highway is nearly whited out, and Bryan slows to fifty, wipers going full blast, fog lamps on for extra light. Even dimmed, the headlights seem to bounce right back from the snow in bright needles. He turns the radio on for the distraction; then decides, after a short corner skid, that he needs to concentrate more, and turns it off. Good thing he knows the road as well as he does.

The snow is slowing, and Bryan can see more clearly, only now there are shapes up ahead and he brakes, slides, grips just in time to fetch up safely behind the last in a line of semis. He's on the incline above the bridge; the line snakes forward ahead of and a little below him, so he can see the white-caked oblongs of vehicles, their tail lights spaced between them.

He can't see the head of the line in the falling snow, but he gets out of the pickup, after a minute or two, and walks up to the truck ahead of him, raps on the door.

Semi jackknifed across the bridge, the driver says. Really wedged in there. Better turn around if you can – my rig's too long.

So there it is. Might as well go back to Roy's. Bryan thinks about calling Lori, even gets out his cell, but then remembers she'd still be at work, not even close to leaving. Not that she's likely to come right home after work, anyway.

He makes a U-turn and heads back north. He almost feels that he should try to get home, but he can't think of an alternate route. Anyway, Roy'll likely be glad to see him, have him spend the night, even. For all he doesn't show it, Roy must be lonely sometimes.

AND NOW ANOTHER MEMORY: It must have been just before they left. A group of hippies camping down by the river, so it was summer. Early summer. Only they weren't really hippies – it was too late in the decade for that. Already 1978, not the Summer of Love anymore, which is when Bryan had been born. Jenny had been hanging around their camp; a couple of times Bryan had come home from school to find her gone from the house, only a note left for him to come there. He hadn't liked it much; the hippies had not been friendly to him, and their children had been mean, too – the older ones bossy, trying to take his stuff off him, the younger ones naked and crusty-nosed. But Jenny had glittered, there, talking, talking, to the men in their long hair and beards. She'd laughed a lot; she'd invited them to come up to the house, to use the shower, to wash diapers. As if it had been her house, Bryan thought: and then, of course it's her house. Hers and Roy's. We all live there now.

Then he'd woken in the night to music, and looked out the window into the backyard, the yard where he played and Jenny said Roy would build him a tree house, the yard that seemed to go back miles, through the meadow and trees, through the whole town, to the river, and there was a bonfire. A bonfire, a big one, half of the winter woodpile they were building, Roy was chainsawing out of trees washed up in the spring flood, piled on it. And people – at first he thought they were strangers, but then he recognized the hippies from the campsite – were dancing around the fire, and they were *naked*.

He'd run to his mom's room, to her and Roy's bedroom, but the bed was empty, not even mussed. Of course Roy was still at work at the station. He could see by the clock that it was just past midnight, so Roy would have just got off the air, wouldn't be home for a few more minutes. And Jenny? He'd run to the window again, and now picked her out, naked as the rest of the dancers, her long hair swinging to her waist, but in no way covering her boobs or her bottom.

What had he done then? He can't remember. Only he must have gone outside, sat on the back porch, because he remembers the stars, and the smell of liquor and the sweetish smoke of the marijuana. The music was coming from Jenny's portable stereo, the one Roy had given her for Christmas.

And then Roy was home, coming out through the back door, stopping, his large body still but not afraid. His hand to his beard. And then the music stopping, so Roy must have turned it off. The dancers all pausing, and then one of them, one of the men (Bryan can see him now, skinny, his long penis hanging) shouting out, mockingly, it had seemed: *Jen, I guess your dad's home.* What had happened next? Bryan doesn't remember. Yes, he does: the hippies gone, with much sarcasm and flipping the bird; shouting, from Jenny and Roy. Himself crying, but unnoticed, swept with them as they moved from room to room, Jenny yelling mean things, Roy responding with heavy – what? Patience, logic, it had seemed to him, then. Not anger.

Himself burning with shame for what Jenny had done.

Back at Roy's, he turns off the engine of his truck but sits still in the cab. Will Roy still be asleep? Will he be willing to let Bryan stay the night?

He imagines Roy nodding, non-committal.

Roy has never asked him about Jenny.

They'd left without Bryan's belongings, in a hurry, on the Greyhound. He'd been so angry at Jenny. Had sulked the whole trip. (Where had they gone? Kamloops, or Merritt: She hadn't had enough money to go further.) She'd said: I should have left you behind. Without turning his face from the window, he'd said: Yes, you should have.

They had slept in a campground just outside of whatever place the bus had dropped them, that first night, on some newspapers and a tarp, Jenny curled around him, her breasts against his back, her breath in his hair. He'd woken to find her gone, to find himself alone in a dark empty place. He knew he'd never see her again.

But then she was back: You're not *crying*, Monkey Man? I just had to take a piss.

And he had thought: How can there be just the two of us? For the first time, he had thought that. He had tucked himself back into Jenny's body, but he had felt, for the first time, that he did not, could not melt into her. That she was too small to hold back the cold, to protect him from the dark, the emptiness, the night sky.

THE
BURGESS
SHALE

CENTRIFUGED OUT OF THE DEPARTMENT by imposed early retirement, out of the Order by heterodoxy, she spins her wheels for one year, two. Her new/old house a shell she maintains, the main tenant. Which is not to say there is no ingress, egress, progress. Mainly, though, regress: reliving, reconsidering, recanting. Then revision: she takes a lodger, who takes her out of herself, takes her places, takes her for granted. She takes exception. The lodger takes it badly, takes it out on her. She takes herself seriously, out of circulation.

This doesn't take her far. She takes more care. Taken. Is it a given? She is given: to fits of despair. Despair fits. (Like a glove? kid? velvet? boxing?) She is boxed in. A boxed set, the sisters, in the Order. Box without a key, house without a door. That old riddle: the egg. To be laid, cracked open? The yolk's on her. She is a soft-bodied creature, defenseless but for her word test, her bone house.

In her new car, her leaving gift from the Order, she drives west, without purpose, at first, along the lakes. Toronto, Thunder Bay. Sleeps at hotels near the Trans-Canada, booked ahead, eats at Zagat-rated places, then doesn't. Swims laps, rises early. Becomes one with the car, her nerve endings fused to wheel, pedal. A disembodied voice, annunciation, updates her on the state of her brake pads.

After Thunder Bay, the dense forest, the open stretches of road. The Cambrian Shield. The speedometer digits metamorphose: 125, 130, 135. The engine, in fifth gear, plainsong in F sharp. The highway a blur of moving water.

Then stubble fields, dusted with the first snow, dotted with gargantuan hay rolls, pumpjacks like Devonian insects. Houses with imitation stone façades. Many collapsing barns. Dozens of hawks: Swainson's, rough-legged, red-tailed, sentinels on power-line posts, hanging in the air over the highway as if at an infinite dining table. The names of hawks rise from her childhood as from a rain-swollen guidebook.

On the salt-rimmed lake at Chaplin, an unlikely pelican, relic of the vast Cambrian Sea. Loving divine pelican. Is there redemption, after a wounding of the self? She sleeps at Super 8s, dreams she is still driving, the highway flowing toward her, a black oleaginous stream.

The salesman from the next table at Roy's Texas Bar and Steakhouse, also alone, also oleaginous. *So, you're an ex-nun?* He says it as if it's the set-up line for an off-colour joke. The line before the punchline. Her knees are pressed together under her high-waisted jeans. But she and the salesman are sitting side by side on his motel-room bed with a bottle of wine inside them and one of Alka-Seltzer on the night stand. She is fifty-seven. She has had sexual congress exactly five times in her life, all in a two-week epoch about six months previously. Her body is reasonably elastic. Her face is still smooth. She is well-preserved. She can pass for fifty, in incandescent light.

She has a horror, now that she has disembarked from that elevated train of post-mortal destinations and joined a more temporal concatenation, of missing out on any important stops.

She says this inside her head and the words, along with the wine, form a little glass case inside which she is able to take off her sweater her pants her grey cotton underwear (grey because it can be thrown in the wash with jeans) and allow parts of herself to be coaxed into temporary, temporal, pliancy.

Her lodger had become presumptuous, had begun to critique her small habits, her devotion to reading: to expect of her the penance of laundry, the benison of prepared meals. She is better off with the temporary, the transient.

After Medicine Hat, she regrets only the small necessary sacrifices: the revelation of her former professions (nun; linguistics professor), her destination (her sister's home in Abbotsford), her name.

From Medicine Hat as far as Banff.

She has spent five days travelling. She stumbles out of the car at her motel, dizzy. It is early afternoon. She could drive further today – reach Revelstoke. She is tempted. But she is tired in her bones, her core. Her tiredness is slowing her momentum; it is a giant elastic band resisting her forward propulsion.

And she has come to the mountains. She has not driven through these passes before. The sight of the slopes and peaks affects her: She is appalled. They are rough, rude, *in extremis*. Naked rock, they jut and thrust.

When she falls asleep, she dreams that she is driving a pass. She dreams that she must feel along the edge of the highway with her hand while she drives, to make sure that she does not go off the edge, down the side of the mountain.

In the morning, her car will not start. She finds a tow truck, a garage, goes exploring on foot.

It is autumn; the aspens of Banff have turned golden. She walks around the downtown, stopping at a wine store, a soap store that censers patchouli and lemongrass into the mountain air for a full block in every direction. She stops at a rock and mineral store selling fossils. She is tempted by a display case of iridescent ammolites. Fossilized nacre: the colours, red, gold, violet, peacock shimmy across the gems' surfaces. But what would she do with them? She does not want to accumulate possessions, weight.

She sorts through all of the buckets in the rock store: She has infinite time on her hands. Fossils from the time before these mountains, for sale.

She walks along the Bow, admiring the brilliant and varied colours of the natural shrubbery. She admires the tumbling waterfall. She crosses a bridge and walks through an old cemetery, where elk are grazing unafraid. She sleeps well, after a dinner of pasta, in her hotel room.

The whorled shells, the world. Time all curled up in its shale strata: the day with its night curving back in reflection; the year with its seasons of burgeoning and decline. The river, the mountains, where once was equatorial sea. We do not visit the same river twice. We do not stand still.

Near here, she knows, lies the Burgess Shale. She has read about and seen images of those obsolete creatures, life forms from half a billion years ago. Records of the other creation. She would like to see the Burgess Shale, to see the fossils in their exposed seabed. This is possible, she discovers. Guided tours, hikes, on-site lectures. She need only drive through the mountains a little more.

She will drive, then, to Field. She will get out of her car, her carapace. She will touch the rock that was mud. She will see the fossils, so tiny, compared to the models in the museum exhibits: squiggles on stone tablets. She will touch the stone bestiary: *Heptogaster*, a coiled, segmented phallus on a little stalk, with carrot-tops branching from its head. *Marrella*, like the rough draft of a trilobite, whose description has it rainbow-coloured. A half-inch long, it would have darted like glossy opalescent fingernails in the warm sea. *Opabinia*, a lush, velvety, lobed worm with a fantail, a proboscis. The famous *Hallucigenia*, with its which-way-up spines, a little handful of jacks, still a mystery. Creatures with bodies like 1950s spaceships, with five eyes or seven legs, with wheels for feet.

Dead ends of evolution, these are, though from the same trees as living creatures. Barren: cloistered nuns.

EN ROUTE AGAIN, she stops at a viewpoint, wrists aching from her grip on the steering wheel. Looks over the view: the rough, scraped, rock. The mountains have buckled up, heaved up against the sea, under which they used to lie. Layers of stone folded back on themselves, thrust up at oblique angles, sliced through. Layers of time, of millennia of microscopic silicate lives, roughly shaken from their sleep at the bottom of the sea, pulled up into the raw air. What are they for, these sterile folds and spills of stone? They are to hold back the continent. They are the continent balking at the sea.

Busses of tourists have also stopped, and the tourists are busy with their raised cellphones, or the telescope lenses of their cumbersome cameras. They crowd near the barriers, but cannot obscure the mountains.

This was the sea. Mud slid, transfixing life, and so we know: life moved. Life moves.

She will gather her resources. She will regroup, repay herself. (In kind? But one is unkind, one is unreachable. One is untrue, one is unteachable. One is unjust and one unimpeachable.)

One is one and all alone, and evermore shall be so.

Alone she stands, but not stock still.

Stasis kills: the anoxic pool.

She will take shelter, make harbour. Harbour resentment, doubts. But also, strangers. Hope. She is wounded, wound up. In her word house she runs round. She will keep time. She will not run down. She will not fossilize: not stand still.

H LY, H LY

HE HAS TO ACCEPT THEIR OFFER, in the end. There's a long weekend, a parade, a sailboat race, besides the university commencement in the city. All of the affordable hotels are full. He can't stomach paying five hundred a night for a hotel room, on top of his flight. He doesn't think he can stomach having to accept their hospitality either, but he really doesn't have a choice.

They give him a bedroom that is clearly the son's – Catherine's son's. Catherine assures him that the boy isn't using it, won't mind. He's working this summer in another province, won't make it home for his sister's graduation ceremony.

Following her down the hallway of the house, which is large and labyrinthine, Kevin tries to think how old the son must be now.

Nineteen! Catherine says. She turns to let him go past her into the room. He was anxious to move out, she says. That's supposed to be the sign you did a good job of raising your kids. If they leave you.

I wouldn't know, he says.

She winces at what he's said, almost imperceptibly.

He wants suddenly to press her up against the wall, to thrust his tongue into her mouth. But the younger daughter is around; he's seen her, a tall thin pale girl, awkward in the doorway. And Catherine's husband will be home soon.

This is what he was afraid of. Why he shouldn't be staying here. He'd had trouble getting out of the taxi, when it had pulled up in front of the house.

She leads him down the hallway, then, to show him the bathroom he'll have to himself. He makes himself focus on her sensibly-dressed person, ahead of him in the hallway. The grey-streaked hair in a bun. The denim shirt and loose cotton trousers. She seems to have lost her high round bottom, since he saw her last. Or maybe it's just that her waist has thickened.

Nevertheless. He feels his cock work upward against the seams of his jeans crotch, feels his senses narrow, sharpen.

She gives him a partial tour of the house. It's a period house, designed by a famous architect a century before. It's not Catherine's house: It belongs to the university and comes with her husband's position. The rooms are high-ceilinged and formal in their geometry, finished in fine, dark-grained wood. The tall windows overlook, to one side, the famous rhododendron gardens, and to another, a sweep of bluebells sloping down to the blue of the sea. The kitchen has been updated, fitted with a restaurant-sized gas stove, several other large stainless steel appliances, acres of gleaming granite.

Catherine bumps his hip with hers. Go on, she says. I know you're lusting after it. Admit it.

Well, yes, he says. A kitchen like this. A chef's fantasy.

It's crazy, Catherine says. Nobody needs a house like this. But shows him the detail of the woodwork, the inlay and groining. He sees the layers, in her: the shyness, intimacy, even of her pleasure in the house's beauty; over that a layer of deprecation, even mockery, at the grandness, the pretentiousness, and another layer over that one, of sensibleness: This is where we have to live. Why pretend?

They have agreed that he will cook, the next night, a really great meal. Of course it's not necessary, Catherine had said. But we'll all love it.

Something convoluted, again: She's doing him a favour, allowing him to repay the debt of their hospitality.

She gives him a house key, tells him to come and go as he pleases, to help himself to anything in the kitchen, to make himself at home. She's businesslike about it. That's Catherine, though: She gives you so much room that you feel you're going to float away.

The truth is he doesn't think about Catherine very much, when he's at home. He has a perfectly adequate life: in comparison to many people he knows, even very fortunate. He and his partner of five years, Aline, have good jobs, mutual interests, a pleasant house. They can afford to eat at a first-rate restaurant once a month, to take a nice trip, in reasonable comfort, every year. They are both, more or less, in good health, and, having met later in life, have no children to cause them anxiety. They considered carefully, before joining their households. They both have good conflict-resolution skills, learned in their respective careers. Aline is a stable, intelligent, self-actualized woman.

It's the longest he's been with one woman. Been faithful to one woman. He carries the fact in him like a secret badge.

What he feels for Catherine – it's the product of conditioning, or body memory. That's all. An inconvenience.

He wishes, futilely, that he had thought of booking a hotel room much earlier.

CATHERINE AND HER HUSBAND have a function to go to this evening, Catherine has told him, apologetically. A *thing*, she said.

Not at all, he said. I have plans with our daughter.

Catherine flustered. With Siobhan! Oh! Great! That's great!

He stays in his borrowed room reading until he hears the call and response of Catherine's and Andrew's voices, the practiced duet of it, cease with the closing of the thick wooden front door, and then takes his spare key and leaves himself.

HE HASN'T SEEN HER FOR six years.

Kevin hadn't even known he had a daughter. Then, ten years ago or more, an email from Catherine. She'd phoned his mother in Bishop's Falls, remembering the name of the place, thinking correctly that it would be the same family. His mother, Mona, had given Catherine his email address, but then telephoned him, cautionary after the fact.

When he'd told Mona he'd found out he had a twelve-year-old daughter, she'd said: She's looking for child support. Ask for a paternity test.

Ridiculous, he'd said. Catherine in her email had brought him up to date, not that he couldn't have found her on the internet anyway. People like her are easy to find out about. For one thing, she must have brought in about twice as much as he did, when he was working. And the husband would be making even more. When he'd said that to Mona, she'd changed her tactic: Maybe you should try to get custody, she said. Then we could sue her for child support. Mona was a piece of work, that was for sure.

He'd had no doubt Siobhan was his: In the pictures Catherine emailed, she looked like his sisters, his mother. The avid overbite, the feral mass of red hair.

Siobhan had not been much interested in him, back then. Catherine had brought her to Ontario, where he lived, to meet him, a couple of years after that email. The two of them had stayed in a hotel and had spent evenings with him, but Siobhan had not seemed much taken with him. He'd proposed a number of outings; he'd polled people he knew, to find out what a girl her age would be interested in. Catherine had suggested a riding school for daytimes, but she didn't want to do anything outside of that except watch TV and message her friends. He'd supposed she had been hoping for a more glamourous father figure, someone dashing who would undermine her parents, take her shopping in Paris, maybe. Instead here was a man with thick fingers and large earlobes, a heavy way of talking when nervous.

She has arrived at the pub with friends, a little disappoint-ment. She looks womanly, now, has filled out a little since he saw her last, has cut and straightened her hair. She's wearing a little business suit, light grey. He understands it's not even Siobhan's own celebration, but an outing of her cohort, her graduating class.

Siobhan and her friends are drinking Jägermeister, that bev-erage of choice for undergraduates even back when he was one himself. He asks the bartender what he has in the way of sin-gle malts. What's your best one? he asks. The bartender takes just a fraction of a second too long to answer, and he is angry, pulls out his billfold and slaps a couple of fifties on the bar.

The bartender says: You want to close your tab now?

No. No he doesn't.

There's Glenlivet. Macallan.

No: something better. How about Bowmore 25-year-old? But they won't have that in a place like this, not at five hun-dred a bottle.

From under the counter, at the back, the barkeep pulls a dusty bottle. He recognizes the name: yes. He'll take two shots of that. One is for Siobhan: Here, he says. See if this isn't better than the Jäg. Let your old man introduce you to the good stuff.

It's thirty-five dollars each for two fingers in a glass.

Siobhan takes a sip, smiles politely. Gulps the rest.

Who is he showing off for? Siobhan seems older than most, but not all, of her cohort. They're all in suits. They've come from some other event. They are children in adults' clothing, he thinks.

From her safe distance, Catherine has kept in touch, updated him frequently. Siobhan had fooled around, gone wild, in her teens. She'd got mixed up with bad boys, had drunk too much, had blown off her classes, dropped out of school. Catherine didn't know what to do with her. He had thought he could tell what she was thinking: his bad genes.

Then, at seventeen, Siobhan had hitchhiked across the country; had arrived unexpectedly, at his house, her red hair bleached copper at the ends from the sun along the Trans-Canada. Wanted him to take her to bars, though she was underage. Had shocked even him with her hooking up, as she had called it.

He'd telephoned Catherine, though Siobhan had said her mom already knew where she was, had let her come. He had felt smug, in some way. Siobhan seemed finally to have decided that there was some point to him. He was to be her ally, the parent figure who understood her, with whom she could be herself, let down her hair. It had taken a lot of moral fibre to discourage this expectation.

He had tried to show this to Catherine, without saying it outright. He had wanted her to recognize that he had done the right things. He'd bought Siobhan a plane ticket back to the coast.

Catherine had said: I'll send you a cheque. Tell me how much.

And then at twenty, Siobhan suddenly moved back home, sobered up, started applying herself, finished her degree on the dean's list. Like a switch being thrown, Catherine had said. He imagined it: a big, two-handed switch, like you might find on an old fashioned railway track.

So, graduating, he says. You're what, a BBA now! Your old man never finished a degree!

He hasn't meant to say that. Tongue like a dead mullet. But Siobhan grins back at him. I know! It's awesome! I finally finished!

But you'll be continuing on?

I don't know. Mum wants me to. But I want a break from school.

You'll get better jobs, he says.

He's thinking he should make some kind of contribution to the group conversation. He does know something about the subject. He reads the papers. In spite of his occupation, he reads, he knows how to think.

He waits for a lull and says: So, what's the doctrine in the business schools these days? Is Greenspan still a saint or is he the devil now?

Blank-faced silence. Then one of the boys, Indian by his look and accent, brightens up and answers him. Oh, that's economics, sir! We don't have to study economics. It's an elective.

Siobhan has asked her neighbour something, he sees. He catches the reply *Macro*. And Siobhan's Jägermeister snort: *Slept through that.*

He'll drink too much, now; he'll flirt too heavily. He'll slip into someone he used to be, and is no longer. He doesn't know why he's here, with Siobhan and her friends.

When Siobhan had arrived at his place, runaway, he hadn't sent her back right away. He'd been on his own, then. It was just before he met Aline. He'd showed her around, cooked elaborate meals, scrabbled through his album and

CD collections for the best jazz and blues pieces to play for her. He'd pulled books from his stacks, made a carefully curated pile for her. Camus, Voltaire, Vonnegut, Nabokov. I'll spare you the Dostoevsky for now, he'd joked.

Siobhan had said to him: I don't want you to give me books to read. Do you understand? I'm not my mother!

Ah, well.

He's thinking it's time to get back to Catherine's. He had not wanted to be there when she got back home from her *thing*, but he doesn't want to disturb the household stumbling back in the early hours of the morning, either.

He finishes his drink and puts the two fifties back on the bar, looks around for a cab phone.

Then Siobhan is pulling him onto the dance floor.

He has never before danced with her. (He can't remember if he ever danced with Catherine.)

The music in his joints and in his spine. He'll pay for it tomorrow, but now it's infusing him; it's permeating his cells. His body thrusts and dips, carves out air according to some blueprint he didn't choose. Some story is moving through him, some arc he must carry out in his shoulders, his pelvis. Siobhan twists in front of him, her face in his, aflame.

Another song and they keep dancing. There's something alive between them, visible to others; he can feel the gazes of the bartender, of Siobhan's friends, astonished, admiring. He can feel the music in her cells as if they were his own. He can feel the music push through her body to speak. They move perfectly together, each balanced and charged, by the other. So that Siobhan's gestures, her responses, are an improvisation on his, and his on hers, and both are illuminated by something new, something sparked out of the music or their affinity. So that they are completely connected, attuned, as if threaded through by a spirit signal. So that they are finally reunited, halves of a whole.

IN THE MORNING his hosts are gone before he wakes up. Catherine has told him they will be off early on Saturday morning, some official capacity to do with commencement. Andrew, Catherine's husband, is some senior administrator at the university, some bigwig: that's why they have this house to live in. Kevin himself needs to go to the market for ingredients for the celebration dinner tonight, which he has promised to cook after the ceremony.

The house is quiet, but with a church-like silence. As if waiting for its purpose. He puts on a bathrobe and finds his way to the kitchen to look for coffee, finds it occupied by Catherine's younger daughter, Anna, with her breakfast and a thick novel. She says, I'll make you coffee. What kind? And almost stumbles, climbing down from the stool. At sixteen, she hasn't grown into her body yet, he thinks. She's taller than Catherine, but has the thin, edgy quality that Catherine had: a sort of nervous flickering.

She puts the new pod in the coffee machine, leaves the used on the counter. He's not a big fan of these automatic expresso machines, but has the same model at home, in his kitchen. Aline had bought it for him, for Christmas.

The girl busies herself with the coffee maker in the way of shy women, as a means of filling up a silence. He reminds himself to be careful with what he says: He likely knows more about Catherine's younger daughter than he ought. What grade is she in now? he asks, though he knows the answer. Where is she thinking about going to university? What bands does she like?

He thinks he's carrying more than his share of the conversation load, but when she gives him the plate of whole wheat toast she's made for him, she looks at him directly under her straight, thick eyebrows (Catherine's eyebrows) and says, sternly: It's nice to take the coffee and the newspaper out to the terrace. And so he is dismissed.

WHEN HE'D HEARD FROM CATHERINE, after all those years, Catherine wouldn't send Siobhan by herself for a visit, and he couldn't afford back then to fly out to the West Coast. But Catherine and he had started to talk: by phone, by email, clandestinely, in part. With pure intentions, and then not. What they'd had before was still there, they agreed, only with the depth and perspective, the grace, of maturity. They made each other happy. They completed each other. They fit together in a way that neither of them did with anyone else.

Then Catherine had flown out with Siobhan and got a hotel room in Thunder Bay, where he was living, and enrolled Siobhan in a riding camp, to give her something to do during the day, while he, Kevin, was supposedly at work. They had had a week of it, of rediscovering each other. They could get back together now, they had said. They had lost all of those years, but things would only be better for it. They were more fully themselves: They would appreciate each other, what they had together, so much more. They had parted like this: They would get back together.

Catherine's two younger children were two and five years old, at that time. She was close to getting tenure. She had not left Andrew, after all.

Still, he waited for her, more or less. For quite some time.

THE COMMENCEMENT CEREMONY is surprisingly religious in aspect. He thinks of church, priests. Medieval-looking robes: the plain black of the graduands, the ornate purple and red and cobalt of the faculty, and their elaborate hats. The program lists a number of ceremonial processes: items carried in and presented formally, doffing and dubbing. An invocation by a First Nations Elder, oddly Christian-sounding.

Earlier, dressed in his suit and waiting for the rest of the family to get ready, he had heard Andrew say to Catherine, rather querulously: I say, aren't you robing, Cathy? And Catherine's reply: Not today, dear.

He's sitting between Catherine and her younger daughter, who says: Is it strange to be in the audience, Mummy? Catherine says, reprovingly: I don't sit on the stage *every year*. I don't even *attend*, every year. He understands this is for his benefit.

Catherine says: It's a lot of hokum, of course. Ritual. I don't know why we keep it up.

But he is moved. Once things get going, he feels it: the weight of tradition, the slowing down of the event with ritual, to make it more important. He respects it.

Siobhan will be the first person in his family to get a university degree.

KEVIN HAS BROUGHT HIS CAMERA, as promised, and, after the ceremony shoots a capacious storage card of images – of his daughter alone, with her friends, various permutations of her family – in the university gardens, among the rhododendrons.

Catherine says: I should take some of you and Siobhan. Just point and shoot?

No. It is not just point and shoot.

He reaches around her to show her how to work the camera. Her nearness. His breath stopping in his ribcage.

Then Andrew, still in his heavy, decorated robes, says: What about the three of you? in a gesture that's either foolish or chivalrous, and so he and Catherine stand in front of some florid bushes with Siobhan between them, both with their arms around Siobhan, as if they had somehow turned back the clock and travelled down a different road.

Catherine has so often over the past years said to him: Andrew is oblivious.

HE'S STANDING NOW IN CATHERINE'S KITCHEN, smiling, listening to the rise and fall of the conversation of Catherine and Andrew, the girls, Siobhan's friends, in the living room, which is two rooms away, through arched doorways. Siobhan has put on one of the compilation CDs he'd made for her when she had last visited: Leonard Cohen, Miles Davis, Nina Simone. Gateway musicians, he had joked: an introduction to the good stuff. The music floats through the archways, sounding very much like music from a decade before.

Siobhan appears in the kitchen doorway. Recognize this?

He appreciates the gesture, smiles at her. May sun slants through the west-facing window, gilding the wood floor, picking up the copper in Siobhan's hair. She's got on a dress that flatters her, bronze silk with a little white collar. In it she looks more demure than the night before, her breasts and hips less flagrant.

That's a pretty dress, he says.

Mummy picked it out for me. She looks uncertain, then, for an instant.

It's very becoming, he says.

I'm not sure it's *me*, she says. But she smiles back at him, and then wraps her arms around him, briefly, kisses his cheek.

He takes the bunch of asparagus out of the shopping bags of food he has brought and removes the band around it. The asparagus spears spray in a fan shape across the cutting board; he gathers them in one sweep of his hand, rinses them and shakes them dry, cuts the ends of the stalks off. The saucepan of water is at a boil; in the asparagus go, for a quick blanching. Twice baptized, they will now be anointed. A splash of truffle oil in the skillet. He shuffles the pan, watching for the slightly translucent shimmer. Then deglazes with a drizzle of balsamic vinegar (oak-coloured, and forty years old). With tongs he lifts the asparagus, still slightly crisp, from its aromatic bed, and wraps it in transparent strips of prosciutto. He arranges the fragrant bundles on a deep-yellow platter he finds in Catherine's cupboard and brings it into the room where the others are gathered. (He likes this platter.) He pours the prosecco. Everyone bites into the hors d'oeuvre with little cries of pleasure. He takes a bundle of asparagus himself.

Yes, he thinks. The flavours distinct, playing off of each other with just the right amount of harmony and antiphony.

He has, for a good reason, no memory of meeting Catherine, and only a couple from their four years of dating and living together. One is of visiting Catherine at her parents' house: She says it must have been the first summer after they met at university, when she went back after term ended. Her parents were away: He and Catherine were alone in the house. He has a strong sensory memory of that house; he can remember the layout of rooms, the colour of the wall-to-wall carpeting, the immense cedars that leaned over the house and kept it in shadow. He and Catherine had made out and then had sex: her first time, not his, but he remembers the shape of her body, her texture and smells and taste, distinctly. The underwater light created by the looming cedars, and the blue-green undertones of Catherine's skin.

The other memory is of a time later, standing in the corridor of their apartment building – Catherine had taken his key, wouldn't let him in their suite – pleading with her to take him back, to give him another chance. The feeling that something inside him was breaking. Catherine nearly softening, but then the apartment door opening, a woman he didn't know asking Catherine: *Is everything alright?* and looking at him with shocking animosity.

He'd deserved it, no doubt about it. At twenty-three he'd been a total fuckup, staying out constantly, coming back to the apartment plastered. Or not coming back, screwing around, not bothering very much at all even to hide it from Catherine.

Now, back in the kitchen, he prepares the soup course: pear-and-leek, which is surprising, seductive, and relatively easy. He puts a pot of stock, made this morning, on to simmer, and chops and cleans the leeks. The leeks go into a little light oil to sauté, and he peels the pears. Then both into the pot of stock for twenty minutes.

He begins to cut up the spaghetti squash and the wild mushrooms. Catherine comes into the kitchen and offers to help, but he sends her out: She will be a distraction.

He'd had a motorcycle accident, in his mid thirties, lost everything. Had to learn to walk and talk again. Lost most of his memories of Catherine, though some had come back, when she'd reminded him of them.

This was the strange part, though. When he'd regained consciousness, after the accident, his first thought had been of Catherine, though he hadn't seen her or heard from her, at that point, for over a decade. He couldn't recall events; it was more that he had a sense that she should be there. He had a sense of her absence. Catherine, and not any of the many other women he'd been with since her, or of the woman he'd been living with just before the accident.

There'd been another accident victim he'd got to know when he'd started his physiotherapy. The guy had lost a leg, just below one knee. He felt the missing leg all the time, he had told Kevin. Phantom limb.

Then Catherine had contacted him. Though she turned out to be married. And to have had his child, and never told him.

He seasons the fish – Chilean sea bass – with *fleur de mer* and a grinding of green and pink, black and white peppercorns.

The fish goes onto thin sheets of softened rice wrapper; he lifts deftly the cubes of fish onto the perfectly square sheets. On each square of fish, he positions a round of mousse that he made earlier that morning with truffles and *foie gras*; it's a strange pinky-black, but smells like paradise. He folds the wrappers precisely – like origami. He lifts the rice wrapper packages one by one into the sauté pan to lightly crisp on each side. His movements are precise and economical.

Not that he could blame her. The time when he was in hospital, when his memory started to come back – that's what he had remembered, his drinking and screwing around. Not in clear detail, but in a sort of montage. It had been a kind of torture, remembering. He could not blame Catherine for ditching him when she found out she was pregnant. No.

He has been faithful to Aline. He feels that for the first time, with Aline, he is doing something honourable. He feels, in this and in other acts, that he may redeem himself.

The pears and leeks are tender. Now, he purées them in the food processor. Catherine and Andrew have a good one, the same make as his. The soup comes out a lovely pale green, sweet and oniony at the same time. He bears it to the table, dippers it into white bowls. Into each bowl he crumbles some dry and veined Stilton. He opens a bottle of *Veuve Cliquot* champagne; it's perfect with the soup, and they all can make toasts: to Siobhan's degree.

The others sit down with cries of amazement this time for the colour of the soup, the clean light taste, the surprise of champagne. It's a shame that champagne is traditionally saved to the end of a meal, he says; its lightness makes it a better wine to begin with. He knows more about wine than most people, though he hopes he's not boring about it.

You should live here and have the use of this kitchen! Catherine says. You deserve it more than I do.

There's no way to answer that.

The fact of Catherine: a sort of permanent ache somewhere in his body. (Not his groin, necessarily, though that is sometimes a pressing issue.) No: the ache is behind his ribs, a little to the right of his breastbone. It's a sort of dry ache, like you get from an empty socket, if you have a less competent dentist. It's the ache of air coming too close to the bone.

He leaves the others having seconds of soup to finish prepping the main course. The squash comes out of the oven; the sea bass goes in. The mushrooms, too, must cook now, in the sauté pan with some olive oil. While they sauté (the brown earthy salty smell rising from the pan like appetite incarnate), he scoops out the flesh of the squash, which separates into tender translucent threads, into a bowl, and dresses it with his own honey-garlic-ginger vinaigrette. He opens two wines for the main course: a 1998 *St. Emilion Grand Cru*, and a bottle of 2000 *Millefiori*. He had spent some time the day before tracking them down.

When Catherine had brought Siobhan to meet him, she had said: We fit together now like two clasped hands. We've been travelling toward each other all this time. It's like we are connected souls.

But he had said only: We have a lot of shared tastes, yes. We fuck nicely, yes. He'd been wary, ungenerous, perhaps.

She had gone back to Andrew, to the other life she had made.

And she had been right to. What is passion, after all? A firing of neurons, triggered by hormones, fuelling, in turn, some stories and images in the mind. Not something real, outside yourself. There's always the point where you choose – where you know, if you have any self-awareness at all – that you're choosing this, making a decision to keep on going, to take this fork in the road. After that point, yes, things get freaky: The brain or heart or whatever it is becomes Pavlov's dog, dissolving willy-nilly into warm body fluids at the sight of the beloved's ass or the sound of her voice. At that point, it's a speeding train, and etc. But before that, a decision.

And then the flood of chemicals subsides; the sensory receptors get dulled. You sit next to the other person and don't get an erection. You get irritated with her over a misplaced receipt and stay mad for three days. You notice the ursine slope of her shoulders, the slurping sounds her tongue makes on the spoon.

It burns off. Or drains off, ebbs away like the water in a flooded basement, leaving, if you're lucky, a crystalline high-tide mark on the walls of memory.

There is no point, now, of changing the shapes of their lives. If there's one thing he has learned since he was twenty-three, since he lost her, it's that sex or lust or romantic love is not everything: that there are many more hours in the day to be filled. There is work; there is companionship. There is self-respect; there is kindness; there are children, aging parents. There is community and food, music. There is making a clean, well-lighted place of life, to borrow a phrase.

At twenty-three he had thought these all shabby imposters, false claimants for his life. But now he has learned that they are all worthy, or none of them is. And Catherine knows this too; perhaps she has always known it. It sounds banal but it is only as banal as daily bread.

The timer goes for the sea bass; it's vital to cook it to just the right point. He pulls out the tray of wrapped, papery packages, which have acquired a varnish like that of an old pine table. Perfect. He punctures one package, carefully; the scents of the cooked bass and truffles and *foie gras* burst out in wisps of steam. The mushrooms are done; he finishes them with a drizzle of the truffle oil, a splash of sherry. He has found a stack of white plates; onto each plate he spreads out a nest of the squash filaments, which are shimmery, opalescent, and then circles the squash nest with the rich loamy mushroom ragout. Then, onto each nest, he lifts tenderly the rice packages. He snips each wrapper so that a small feather of steam ventures, a spirit messenger. He carries his offering to the table.

You are an artist, Kevin, Andrew says, his hands together, his pink head shining faintly, priestly, even in his ordinary clothes.

You either believe or you don't believe, maybe. You see that possibility as real, transcending and preemptive of normal experience, normal rules. You believe that falling in love with the one right person will transform and hallow your life forever, or you don't believe that. If you believe it, you will think it worth any price. And if you don't believe in it – well. You'll have a much more stable life. You'll wake up every day, grateful that the wool hasn't been pulled over your eyes. That you haven't risked – or lost – everything. You'll wake up grateful for that every day.

For dessert, a lemon tart, a bottle of Californian orange Muscat.

From across the table Catherine's face: soft, astonished, bewildered.

HIS RETURN FLIGHT isn't until Sunday afternoon, and, waking Sunday morning, he wishes he'd scheduled the flight earlier. He has no idea what he's going to do with this day. But before he can bring himself to get up, there's a tapping at his door, and Catherine comes in, wearing something that isn't quite a bathrobe, her hair on her shoulders. She's carrying a mug of coffee that he can smell is real.

Andrew is out, she says: He's running a half-marathon. Anna sleeps in on Sundays, she says, but Catherine herself is an early riser. She likes the unspoiled morning.

He growls: Lock that door. I want to take you right now.

He doesn't know why he says this.

She smiles; she sits on the edge of the bed. She bends over him, wraps her arms around his neck, kisses him on the mouth, deeply, slowly.

The flesh of her upper arms hangs loosely, now, and her small nose and mouth disappear in flesh when she leans forward, but he does not close his eyes.

There is no strangeness between them, only comfort, only familiarity. She lays her head on his chest, for a few moments. He strokes her hair. She sighs.

Catherine slides her body down beside his and puts one leg over his thigh. She props herself on her elbow and gazes into his eyes. What is that? A flicker, an unextinguished match tossed, he thinks. He hears her thought: Perhaps we could have this. Perhaps it would not cost everything. Perhaps it wouldn't burn itself out.

He grips her hair in his hand, tightens his grip. This too is a sign between them. Scent of roses, wine on the tongue. The prerogative of the invisible. Okay, he says. *Holy*. Okay now. Okay.

THE BIRDS
OF INDIA

SHE'S THE FIRST TO ARRIVE at the airport. Peter drops her off on his way to work, hefting her suitcase and giving her an unexpected hug. *Ow, ow,* she says. Her upper arm is still sore from the last of the injections. He pats her bottom as if it's a neighbour's dog, a little mechanically, but with general goodwill.

Then he's gone, the truck disappearing behind the smoke-screen of its own condensation-filled exhaust. She goes through the large automatic doors quickly. It's January, and she's left her parka in Peter's truck.

Vancouver, New Delhi, the ticket agent says, and she feels a little rush of the importance of this trip. Not many people must be flying that route today, from this little airport. "I wonder if my friend Charlotte has checked in yet?" she asks, though she knows it's much too early. The ticket agent says,

"No, none of the other passengers continuing on to India have checked in yet." She wants to tell the agent why she is going, she wants to be asked, but the agent does not make an opening, and there are other passengers lined up behind her, and so she does not say anything, though it is bubbling up inside her.

She'll kill some time in the coffee shop. She means to have only a cup of coffee, but ends up eating a second breakfast, in spite of her New Year's resolution. The date muffins look so good, and who knows when she'll get another meal? She takes a table positioned to see the rest of the airport, so she can watch for the others. Likely they'll come in for coffee as well.

But they do not, and when her flight is finally called, and she goes through the security check and into the boarding lounge, they're already there, standing in a little group.

So she is the last to arrive, instead of the first.

And there is Charlotte, reassuringly. She doesn't know any of the others. Charlotte is talking to a tall man with silver hair and a little silver earring, but says, Ah, there you are, and introduces her. It's the group leader, Henry, who will be shepherding them all of this trip.

Henry asks, Was it difficult to rise so early this morning? She starts to answer that she's up early every morning, getting Peter's breakfast, but his eyes lose focus, drift slightly sideways, almost instantly, to gaze around the airport, though he almost instantly recalls himself, places his attention back on her with professional discipline.

Her tongue falters then, her cheeks warm with embarrassment. He's a handsome man, lean, with well-proportioned features. Very handsome. His voice is deep and resonant, a singer's. He's casually but elegantly dressed in a light linen blazer, a very fine cashmere pullover, trousers that are not khakis or jeans but something else, something matte and crisp. Peter does not own anything like these clothes. He wouldn't have any occasion to wear them. From Charlotte's description, she had imagined Henry in some sort of uniform: tan gabardine, a badge on the shirt.

She sees herself in his eyes, a middle-aged woman, a little fleshy, sensibly dressed in grey no-iron pants and a blue flowered shirt. As always, a little less glamorous than Charlotte, a lesser replica: a little shorter, a little fatter, a little less fashionable. Charlotte has on some sort of tunic sweater and leggings, in shades of taupe. Is her outfit too stylish for the occasion?

Your outfit looks comfortable for travelling, she says to counter her critical thought. Charlotte is thinner, since her illness. Her hair has grown in nicely, though, and swings in a honey-brown wing near her jaw. Charlotte grimaces, slightly. She has said the wrong thing, again. She had once asked Charlotte for the name of her hairdresser, and had gone herself. She had come out with a hairstyle that had transformed her for about two days, until she had washed it, and not been able to get it to fall in the same way. She'd had a colouring, too, layers of tinfoil lowlights and highlight, and she has to admit it looked natural, and didn't show roots as quickly, but she couldn't justify the price, when she could buy a box of L'Oréal at the drugstore for twelve dollars.

But Charlotte is saying now, Vicki and I worked in pediatrics together. Vicki has such a lovely touch with children. Ah then, Henry says, You'll lose your heart to our Centre.

She had been head of pediatrics for several years, has just retired from nursing. She waits for Charlotte to say something about this. It is her expertise that has brought her on this trip.

Something about the way Charlotte is standing. At their age. What they are offering now is their labour, their generosity, their expertise. Their wisdom.

SHE HAS HEARD ABOUT THE HEAT, the smells, the noise, but in fact the Delhi airport could be any very large airport, and they step from its shining air-conditioned corridors into a perfectly modern air-conditioned bus and then are whisked to a perfectly modern air-conditioned hotel. They could be anywhere. She sleeps heavily in the room she shares with Charlotte. In the morning, though, Charlotte is wan, a little edgy.

Did you not sleep? she asks, and Charlotte pulls her lips up almost sarcastically.

The jet lag, probably.

Once they arrive at the Centre, she minds, at first, when she finds out that she is to fill the days taking her turn at cooking – which mostly seems to be carrying water and washing and cutting up vegetables – rather than work as a pediatric nurse, as she has been trained to do. She had thought, when Charlotte had told her about the trip, a mission for children in India, that they'd be doing medical work with the children, but in fact there are young doctors and nurses here who are doing that. She doesn't so much as hold a baby. Charlotte isn't doing nursing work either. Rather, she seems to be busy with Henry, who is, apparently, not really in charge, as there is a

Director, a small, dignified, silver-haired Indian man. Of the rest of their group, some are put to work in the garden – in which weeds seem to grow foot-high overnight – and others are put to work on a new hospital structure. There are engineers, professional builders, who have also volunteered their time, she understands. Their group members, though some of them are experienced builders, too, carry lumber and bricks and plaster. If Peter had come, he'd be frustrated – he'd be put to work as a labourer. There's some sort of inefficiency here. She tries to talk to Charlotte about it, but Charlotte spends her days at Henry's elbow, doing paperwork and taking minutes at meetings.

The vegetable chopping and water carrying fills the time. She's learned to get up very early, when it's not so hot yet, and start her chores. The other workers are also mostly awake and on the move. She doesn't leave the clinic compound: doesn't venture further than the compound farm with its ancient trucks, the cinder-block and corrugated tin buildings. The land is dry here, like back home: bare hills with scrubby, prickly trees, sparsely distributed, but she doesn't venture out of the Centre. She walks as far as a large banyan that seems to have faces in its braided trunk – at least, she sees them out of the corner of her eye, though when she focuses on them more squarely, they're gone.

She feels that she is experiencing everything through smudged glass. It might be the anti-malaria drugs.

In the evenings, in her fifteen-minute allotment of computer time, she emails Peter, and sometimes CCs their sons, Mark and Cory, if she feels she's put more effort than usual into the message. She describes the birds, which she has begun to identify – Henry has loaned her a book, or rather borrowed one from the elderly doctor who runs the clinic. *Peepel, mynah,* she writes. She doesn't know if Peter is interested, but she knows he can name the hawks that they see around Kamloops. She describes the farming practices and implements, sometimes with, she thinks, a fair bit of skill. One evening she writes to Peter, I do not know why I'm here. Maybe I should try to get a flight home sooner. She doesn't send the email, though.

She feels that she is floating, disembodied, invisible.

She shares a small room with an elderly Indian woman who also works in the kitchen, and who doesn't speak much English, but who has some status that sets her apart from the other Indians who work for the clinic, the locals. She was supposed to share with Charlotte, but Charlotte had asked to be moved. You snore, Vicki, Charlotte had said.

She had chosen not to be hurt. She knows she snores. It's her weight, and the dust, which aggravates her allergies. And Charlotte is still not really well, though she looks better now that she has tanned a little.

One day there is an expedition for their group to a nearby bird sanctuary, a famous one where hundreds of species of migratory birds stop. Some of the French doctors and nurses who are volunteering go too – but not Charlotte.

At the park gates there are bicycles to rent by the hour, but they are in an advanced state of disrepair. Instead, it seems, they must hire bicycle rickshaws pedalled by very thin Indian men who seem either very young or very old. None of the rest of the group invites her to share a rickshaw, but a middle-aged German couple in shorts and hiking boots offers her a ride. She climbs in. It will be a three-hour tour. Their driver has a long name that sounds like a little creek flowing over rocks, but which she forgets instantly. He says that he is called number forty-two, anyway. He is supposed to identify all of the birds and other wildlife they come across. There are few birds. The sea of shimmering water, the 350 species of local and migratory birds promised by the travel guides, do not materialize. What they do see are peafowl, and water birds like moorhens and widgeons that she might see on any pond back home.

The Germans, who sport a checklist, express their dismay twenty minutes into the trip. They want to see exotic birds. More birds appear, gradually – egrets, cormorants, eagles, herons. Bitterns and swallows. The rickshaw driver points them out. The Germans seem somewhat appeased.

She tries to remember them for Peter. She has forgotten to bring the bird guide loaned to her by the Director. The Germans offer her their high-powered binoculars with formal courtesy, but she doesn't really care, she finds.

No Siberian Crane? the male German curtly asks their driver, who responds with a combined glibness and half-hearted optimism, Oh, yes, sir: just not visible today, sorry, sir. Their exchange so layered with pretense and distrust as to sound diplomatic.

A hammering grows and fades as they bump around the lake path: diesel pumps, she sees, sputtering water from tattered hoses into muddy pools. The driver explains. There is a drought: The monsoon has not yet come, this year. Villagers are diverting water from the park for their own uses. He tells them a long, angry story about a riot the week before: villages clashing over a rumour, intentionally started, that a new irrigation pond would be dug in a graveyard.

There will always be droughts. What is important: the welfare of thousands of villagers, or of thousands of migratory bird species? She is not sure. No ibis, no spoonbill, no hornbill, the German woman observes, as if she will fail an important exam.

Snakebird, the driver says, pointing. Very rare. There is a bird, or rather the long, yellow-pink extended neck of a bird cutting through a pool of water. The water is opaque, café au lait; the bird's face sharp-billed, with turquoise cheek patches. The rest of the bird is invisible under the water. The Germans have a discussion, express doubt, it sounds like, over the rarity. She writes the name of the bird down anyway. She cannot tell what is important, or real, anymore.

When they return to the park entrance, the French doctors and nurses getting out of their rickshaws claim to have spotted a python, a monitor lizard, a tiger. The German man pats Vicki's shoulder. No tiger for us, he says, sympathetically, as if the three of them have, deservedly, been denied a treat. It is the first time she has been touched in a week. She can feel the warmth of the man's hand, a tactile afterimage, even after they get back on the bus.

Kein Eden, the German man says, sadly, but perhaps not disapprovingly.

ANOTHER OUTING, finally, to a nearby town. The minibus is not air-conditioned, but the windows are wide open: it roars and grinds though streets that are strewn with objects, as if the buildings have turned inside out. For a few blocks, children run alongside, grabbing at the bus, calling, the whites of their eyes flashing. On the bus, there is a strong smell of body odour. The woman beside her says, desperately, I'm going to be sick, and then is sick, on the floor beside Vicki's feet. In spite of her years of dealing dispassionately with body emissions, nausea rises in her.

Stumbling out of the bus, she is assaulted by the heat and racket and smells – like every smell in the world, pleasant and unpleasant: cooked meat and scorched vegetables; garlic, cumin, chili; excrement – human, cow and chicken; urine, sweat; smoke, sewer, petroleum – both combusted and not; soap, vinegar, ammonia. And every sound – mechanical, human, animal, musical, industrial – has been mixed together in a cacophony. The heat is overwhelming. She has got used to heat at the clinic, but this is something else. She is wearing a tank top meant for layering, and has cut off the legs of her trousers, not caring any longer about her flabby upper arms and varicose veins, but now, out in the heat of the day, she is drenched in sweat. Perspiration runs down her sides and her backbone, pooling under her breasts and the top of her rump.

She stands in a narrow segment of shade shared by a rooster and a goat, blank, waiting. Six more weeks. She should buy something – a shawl, jewelry, a carving of an elephant. But then their driver appears out of nowhere to chivvy them back into the bus. Something has happened – some catastrophe, personal or political, she can't be sure which. A visit to a local palace, also, is inexplicably cancelled. That is, there are several explanations, but they contradict each other. There is no authoritative word.

AT NIGHT the longing for home rises like the phantom pain of a missing limb. She thinks: It is because I see so little of Charlotte. She tries not to resent that, not to think about how Charlotte had talked her into this trip, how she'd envisioned the two of them sharing a room, working side by side during the day in the children's hospital wing, as they had done, twenty-five years ago, as new-fledged nurses. She tries not to resent this, but it is hard.

And she had not wanted to undertake this expensive trip to India. She had come for Charlotte, to be with Charlotte, who had almost died last year and who was her best and oldest friend.

But she sees now that the only possible justification for this trip is that it be a spiritual journey, a pilgrimage of letting go, and so she must not resent any deprivation.

The elderly Indian woman, Gita, snores, too. Gita, who is older and greyer and saggier than herself, even, smiling, rolling into the room like a smudge of sweet incense, pressing her palms together and bowing a little, *Namaste*. She had thought: Gita will be my consolation. She will show me by her example how to submit gracefully, to have no expectations. But Gita is a dictator, fierce and intransigent about the way to make up the inadequate cots, how to stow her toothbrush in the tin mug on the room's lone shelf. Gita has a coloured photocopy print of Mother Theresa pinned to the wall above her cot, and Vicki had wondered if she were a nun, but she doesn't seem religious.

She showed Vicki how to bathe, in the really Spartan set-up. They don't get to shower every day – only the French medical workers do. And Gita showed her how to roll her shirt up and then down, to scrub away at her high-smelling crevices with a rag, soap, not very warm water. It's all in the order you do it, the woman mimed. Face, breasts, arms, pubic area, feet last.

She does not feel clean. She looks forward to her twice-weekly shower as the compound garden to its watering. She ceases minding exposing her doughy, freckled self in the open cubicles. In the shower, she feels, for a few moments, contained in her own skin.

CHARLOTTE COMES AND FINDS her in her room. She and Henry are going back to Delhi for a few days. It's the heat or her tiredness, but Vicki can't process the information right away. What is Charlotte saying? Then she says: Oh, take me with you.

No, Charlotte says. You can't come.

Something like a heat devil dances where she ought to be comprehending, manifesting in her facial expression. You needn't scowl at me, Charlotte says. I'm sure you'll be alright for a couple of days without me.

The tone Charlotte has used is condescending, snotty. Vicki feels a kind of shock travel under her skin. She stares, involuntarily, at her friend. Her streaked hair, her light golden tan, the translucent skin under her eyes, her teeth, which all, inexplicably, have little metal rims at the gum line, the deep lines radiating along her top lip. Vicki has an urge to slap Charlotte, wants to knock her over, all five foot nine of her, kneel on her chest, tear out her silly dangly silver hoops, grip her burnt-blonde hair in her fists and bang her head up and down on the chipped and cracked concrete floor.

Why is she here? She tries to remember – what had Charlotte actually said, when she had told Vicki about the trip? She had thought it was, I'm going on another service mission to India – you should come. But maybe it had not been that at all. She wonders suddenly what she is paying for out of the quite hefty residence fee. She hasn't seen a breakdown of that fee. It occurs to her that India is supposed to be cheap, and for what she's paying, she could probably be staying at a luxury resort in Thailand or Bali. She hadn't told Peter what the trip cost, and he hadn't asked, just said, *Go for it!* She feels now a little shame, that she hadn't told him the particulars, that he had assumed she knew what she was doing.

Had Charlotte invited her, or had she invited herself along? What is she doing here?

A COUPLE OF NIGHTS LATER, when Vicki returns to her room, after cleaning up the last meal service, Gita conveys through sign language that Henry has a message for her. Are they back, then? But when she goes and finds him in his office, he puts his hand over hers and says, I am sorry your friend is ill. I am hoping the hospital in Delhi will help her.

Again, the shock under her skin. She feels suddenly light and small, as if she might blow away. Charlotte is ill, then?

She's in the hospital, in Delhi, for diagnosis. She's had some symptoms. Henry pats her hand. No need to talk. You will let it go better by not talking, hmmm?

Well, that's certainly contrary to the wisdom of the western world. But in her narrow bed, she thinks about how much talking goes on: about how much she herself talks, effortlessly, endlessly, as if she's pouring a lubricant out onto all and everything around her. She is a talker; she will be the first to admit that. But she's always seen it as a grace, an effortless action, like breathing. Now small silences of others light up in her mind, a whole lifetime's worth. Does she talk too much? Do people resent her talking? She is not mean-mouthed, like some other people back home. She doesn't gossip or complain.

She feels a strike, like a snake's, at her core, at some organ in her centre. Charlotte's defection, her busyness, not just here but at home as well. Peter's long working hours, his letting her travel without remonstrance. Her sons' independence. Are they all just sick of her? Have they all been wishing just to be rid of her?

In her lumpy cot she lies awake, her molecules disintegrating, her outlines dissolving.

The next day as she's helping to prepare the evening meal, Henry comes and finds her and talks to her in the high-ceilinged, blue-painted hall, with its scrubbed plain tables and floor. Charlotte has to be flown home, he says, before she's too ill to travel. Do you want to leave with her? She will need some help getting through the airports and so on.

Her first thought, even before alarm for Charlotte, is a dismay that shocks her. Leave now, when she has two weeks to go! But she has wanted to leave, has fixed her energy on leaving, from the moment she arrived.

And what is wrong with Charlotte? She feels a sense of shame, asking Henry, which is not mitigated by the surprised glance he gives her, nor his explanation, nor the shock she feels at the news.

How had she not known? And then she hears herself start to babble, Oh, typical Charlotte, so brave and what a grand gesture, so unselfish. But her face is growing hot: She can feel the blood pumping to her cheeks, and with it some anger, caustic, burning. And she must shut her mouth, she must press her fingers to her lips, and walk out of the cool quiet blue room very quickly, and into her own room, where she sits on her bed and shuts her eyes and slows her own breath with her will.

How had she not known? And why had Charlotte not told her? Self-reproach and anger at Charlotte course through her, now – not simultaneously, but alternating, one on the heels of the other, as if they were fountains of sludge bubbling in her, somewhere around her upper thoracic area, and she sees herself, a foul machine like the incinerators attached to the clinic, burning rubbish beneath, toxic invisible gases pouring from her mouth. *Unclean, unclean,* she wants to cry.

Vicki does not fly home early, with Charlotte. Instead, Charlotte's two daughters fly to India to retrieve their mother, take her home. Vicki doesn't see Charlotte – she is only able to render service by packing Charlotte's suitcases, which are then taken into Delhi by the group of French doctors and nurses returning to Europe. Charlotte is dead, by the time Vicki returns to Canada.

During her last two weeks she is moved out of the kitchen and into Charlotte's position as Henry's assistant. This is at once more interesting and more demanding than her kitchen work, but she does not think it more fulfilling, as she had imagined it must be. Her envy at Charlotte's spending time with Henry – she recognizes it as envy, now – seems a foolish thing. When she suggests to Henry that one of the others in their group – Helen, who is a retired accountant, or Jim, a lawyer – might be better at the job, he uncharacteristically wrinkles his face, shakes his head and lets out a quick involuntary *no*!, then recovers himself and says that Helen and Jim are too useful to the building team to be switched.

One of her duties is to work on a narrative report that Henry must submit yearly, and in reading past reports and working on this report she deduces (not to her surprise, no – but not to any satisfaction at the confirmation of her suspicions, either) that Henry has a very interesting position vis-à-vis the clinic and the Centre: that is, it is not apparent what he does besides bring small groups of women – mostly women, and mostly, she thinks (from their limited contributions) retired, middle-aged women, but also some younger people, especially younger men – to the Centre for eight-week stints, for which experience they pay inordinate sums of money. Some of this money goes toward the Centre, but much of it – and sums collected from individuals who do not choose to travel here – go, as far as she can see, toward Henry's travels back and forth from India to various parts of Canada, four times a year, and his living expenses while in Canada.

She does not see any financial records, of course. She sees only the reports, and gathers, from what she has paid herself, from what little Charlotte had told her, what is going on. She is not shocked at the revelations about Henry's "work." She has somehow lost the ability to be shocked, she thinks, by the time she has figured out this story. She is not shocked at Henry's duplicity, his audacity. She is not admiring of it, either. She will not tell Peter, she thinks. Then she thinks that she will tell him – that she will require more honesty, more transparency, of herself. Then she decides, again, that she will not tell him. He does not need this knowledge. It can do him no good. She wonders if she should report it to someone – but who? And what would she be reporting, after all? She thinks that the Director of the Centre must have some idea, must be content to take the small amount of the recruits' work and money that Henry remits, and may not want to lose even that.

She understands, from the work that Charlotte has already done, in her series of trips, from her years of knowledge of Charlotte, that her friend also must have read this story and comprehended it fully.

THERE IS A SHORT STAY in Goa on the way back. Charlotte had booked this part of the trip for them, and Vicki does not know how to unbook it, so she must go, with Henry and a couple of the other people who travelled with them. The hotel seems unnecessarily luxurious, next to the clinic. We need this, to recover our strength for the work ahead of us, Henry says. And she understands, from her work on the report, that Henry cannot stay in this nice hotel in Goa on the way home unless others do as well – that he is expected to see them back to Kamloops. So though she would much rather go straight home, not spend three more days, she does not protest, but accepts what has been booked for her, out of her money.

She walks by herself, though, looking at the birds, the everyday birds, spotted doves and mynahs that had flown in and out of the kitchen in the Centre. She walks past the tourist shops with their racks of cheap rayon shirts and dresses, their shelves of boxed papaya and cashews, of faux bronze Ganesha statues and silver jewelry, suntan lotion and thongs. She walks by the enormously expensive shops, with their handbags whose cost would feed and house an Indian family for a year. In a crosswalk she hears a man trying to sell another man a gram of something unnamed for $60 US. She passes thin children selling CDs of sitar music, with as little interest as she would have in a plaza parking lot in Kamloops.

On their last day in Goa, Henry hires a car and driver and takes her – just her, not the others – to dinner. Henry is looking very sleek, she thinks. He smells of licorice and aloes and something floral – hibiscus, maybe. What have you been doing with yourself? she asks, and then wishes she hadn't. An odd expression flits across Henry's face. Indulgence, she'd call it. At the same time, his lips curl slightly. That would be what is called a sensual smile, she thinks, though she does not know if she has seen one before. She does not speak.

You are sad, Henry says. They are on the top floor of a hotel, on a terrace that is roofed with palm fronds under which large fan blades turn endlessly. Below them are the city's lush gardens and lights, the band of sand and sea, the waves sweeping endlessly onto the shore, and endlessly retreating.

Henry says, You are sad to be leaving India, Vicki. But don't be. You did a lot of good work. You made a difference. And you can come back. The clinic would welcome someone of your calibre every year.

She says nothing. Henry has moved his chair so that they are seated side by side, now, looking at the view. He puts his hand on her arm. She looks at it: his tanned, freshly manicured fingers. I know what you're feeling, Henry says. Your heart is still there with those tiny ones. You have something exceptional to offer, Vicki. You're thinking, why not commit to another eight weeks next year?

A sound almost like a giggle nearly escapes her. If Peter could see this! But she sobers, remembering she can't even begin to tell him.

I think, Henry says, and he slides his fingers down her arm and intertwines them with hers, I think you and I are alike. We need to give, but we need constraints, or we'd give everything we have, and that would be the end of us. That's why I can't let you come back, Vicki. I know you want to do more. You and I, we have that compulsion. But I can't let you spend – expend – everything you have.

She's about to speak, then, to say that she'd love to come back to the clinic, if they'd only let her work with the children, but Henry puts his finger on her lips, tenderly, so that what comes out of her mouth is a muffled bleat: *Mmunh*.

Yes, money, Henry says, sadly. It's never a substitute for the real thing, is it? But sometimes it has to do. Sometimes, it's all we can do. And then, I think, it's an acceptable sacrifice.

In her mind her voice is babbling away: *Well, you know, Peter and I don't have a lot, though we've worked hard, but we've got a little put away, I suppose more than we actually need....* Babbling, bubbling away, and underneath, that hot element of anger she never used to notice. But she doesn't open her mouth: She doesn't speak. She watches, instead, the brazier, burning away smokily in that great blue room. Charlotte is dead now, leaving with her secrets. Peter has called her, actually made an international call to the hotel to let her know. She had loved Charlotte. Perhaps. She had also envied her, for decades her envy like a bird with the head of a snake, swimming under the water.

But she had used Charlotte's name, on the envelope of Henry's accounts and receipts that she slipped into Helen's room at the hotel, an envelope of items meant to be shredded, but perhaps very meaningful to someone in Helen's profession.

She knows that she has not been motivated by a strong sense of ethics in giving those documents to Helen.

She pulls her fingers, gently, from Henry's grasp, lays them over her purse, which is in her lap. She feels her lips tighten into a thin line. Something has hardened inside her. But she can feel the ground, at last. Even though she is in a sort of limbo in this tropical paradise, she can now feel the ground.

The fan blades whir, and stutter, occasionally. The lights flicker: the twinkling lights of the city, as well. The power is not consistent, Henry says. She can see that.

The air is warm milk, or warm silk, something too soft and slippery to trust.

When she gets home it will be March, and the worst of winter over, but the landscape will be bare and sere, hiding nothing, pretending nothing. She will be glad to be home.

INSTANT

They're still working on the basement. Leslie's supposed to be giving Jonelle a break by watching Jackson for the morning. She had thought, eight o'clock, but Mike had laughed. Nobody up around here till at least ten. Come then.

She's kind of shocked. Their dad would have had them up at six on a Saturday morning. Chores, paper routes. It's how you get ahead, he'd said. She still can't sleep past six, even if she wants to, even the time she went on vacation with friends to Vegas. Her body has a built-in alarm clock. But look how much more you can get done.

You've got a new haircut, Jonelle says in a kind of squeal.

Yeah. Thanks, Les says. Then feels something flag inside her: it wasn't a compliment.

Her hair, the deep fox-red locks of it on the floor of the beauty parlour, already dulled, like a dead animal. Her head feels like something shameful, now: a body part not meant to be seen.

She had not meant to have it all off. She had woken a few mornings ago, feeling it greasy, disgusting. Well, it was a bother, at work. Whether to put it in a pony tail or what. Had imagined something clean, angular. It was only later, in the chair, when she'd got into that little argument with the hairdresser, that she'd decided: Cut it all off. All of it.

Pixie-bob, the girl had said. That isn't a thing. But it was. She'd seen pictures on Pinterest. That's what they called it.

Got it all buzzed, she says. Easier to take care of. No fussing.

It's striking, Jonelle says, nodding. Hardly any pause, as if she wasn't searching for a word.

They are in the kitchen. Jackson is at the table, a mess of Cheerios and banana, like some sort of aggregate spill has happened. Shouldn't a three-year-old be able to feed himself more efficiently? Also, it's ten-thirty already. She'd expected him to be ready to go at ten. But no.

Jonelle herself still in pajamas. Keegan was up in the night, she says. She yawns. She doesn't seem to possess any forward momentum.

Teething? Les asks. Sympathy, not judgment: that's what she is cultivating here.

Jonelle laughs. Teething! He's only two months old.

Well, what does Leslie know? She's never been around a very young baby before. She hadn't really been in Mike's life when Jackson was born.

Might not be now, except that Jonelle had apparently insisted on meeting her, had kept inviting her over, even when Jonelle and Mike were still living in Jonelle's parents' basement. Had invited her to holiday dinners with her own family, even.

Mike's eyes: don't mess this up for me.

So she was careful. Said nothing. Didn't drink, just in case. People like Jonelle had rules that you couldn't guess existed: weird rules that could ambush you just when you felt most at ease. She knew that.

Jonelle wasn't what she had expected Mike to end up with. Nope. She'd imagined the kind of girl who took pins to condoms. But Jonelle had a college degree, worked in a bank, had paid mat leave. Paid. Right now, sitting in that chair, hair in her eyes, yawning, she's getting paid.

No wonder Mike toes the line, these days.

She hears a kind of static fuzz in the back of her head. Jackson, you look like you're finished, she says. She knows she's said this about three times already, to no effect. Don't you want to go to the park with Aunty?

Aunt Leslie's going to take you to the park, Jonelle says, as if translating. Can you drink up your milk now and get dressed?

There's the sound of hammering from downstairs and then the thin wail of the baby. Jonelle swears, lifts herself up as if she's a hundred, heads for the back bedroom.

At this rate, they're never going to get out the door. Les takes Jackson by his elbows, which seem the least encrusted part of him, lifts him onto the floor.

He shakes his head. She begins to steer him down the hall, toward the bathroom. No, he says. No. But she pops him up on the stepstool, anyway, turns on the tap, begins to scrub him down. Avoids his eyes in the vanity mirror.

Don't you want to see the animals?

No, he says.

She steers him to his bedroom, which is decorated with a stick-on mural of realistic animals – giraffes, hippopotami, some sort of monkeys, a lion – and begins opening drawers. Pants, sweater, socks. There are tiny y-front underwear in a drawer but some sort of pull-on diaper on top of the dresser. Which? Diaper, she decides.

When they go back to the kitchen, Jonelle is in the chair again, her pajama top pulled up, the baby latched onto her. Jonelle's boob is bigger by some than Keegan's bald round head. He's all body, like some sort of sucking parasite, his stumpy useless arms and legs folded in on him. Les feels a little ill, has to look away.

Her nephews. Her blood. She has to forge a relationship. Whatever it takes.

Now Jackson says he wants to go downstairs, to see his dad. But she's here to keep him out of Mike's way, while he's working. You don't want to go down there, she says, moving towards the door to keep it shut.

But Jackson, the little monkey, has the basement door open. Dad! he calls. Daddy!

That brings Mike up the stairs. What's up, Tiger?

Then, looking at Les: Jeez Louise: Did you fall under a mower?

The sting of it. But that's how she and Mike talk to each other. Just not usually around Jonelle, right? It's on her no-fly list, that kind of kidding.

Now Jackson says he doesn't want to go out; he wants to stay and watch Daddy.

She doesn't want to go out now, herself. But she's geared up for it. Half the morning gone already. And just to walk to the park, where she'll push Jackson on the swing and try to make him look at the pot-bellied pigs. She'd wanted to make a day trip to the wildlife park, but that was also a no-fly with Jonelle. And Mike too, if she is honest.

It's going to be fun, Mike says. Aunty Leslie will make sure you have fun.

Jonelle says, Jackson, can you please make sure you hold Aunt Leslie's hand when you cross the street?

Okay. That's meant for her. She gives Jonelle a mock salute from the doorway. Then spies Mike's prized Jets cap on a peg, flips it onto her own shorn head.

JULY

Sheila the HR person says, So, Leslie, lots better feedback the last two weeks.

As if it's not really *lots*. As if *lots* is a word that means something else, like something so miniscule there isn't a name for it. As if the feedback is something separate from Sheila, not the forms she's having Larry and the others fill out on Leslie every day.

There had better be good feedback. She has tried.

It's six weeks now. She's halfway there.

These last two weeks she has tried very hard to do what Sheila has shown her, in the training videos she makes Leslie watch in an empty office while she, Sheila, is next door, presumably, at her desk. She has tried to Put Herself in the Resident's Shoes, to Use the You-Perspective, to Make a Personal Connection, to De-personalize and Defuse Conflict Potential, to Practice Perfect Protocol, to Communicate, Collaborate, and Conciliate.

All of this she has to do at a counter, a cashier's wicket, where she mostly collects fines and stamps receipts, and at her desk, where she tries to find things in a computer system that makes absolutely no sense.

So, any questions? Sheila asks.

The way Sheila smiles: Her face doesn't open up and make you relax, like when most people smile, but instead it seems to close down, like the jointed metal screens they can pull down over their wickets. She wants to ask Sheila: Do they teach you to smile like that at business school? Because she has seen Jonelle do it too.

Not that Sheila is a bit like Jonelle. What you get with Sheila is some kind of hard metal box. You can't see what's inside. Jonelle is soft, soft. Only a little hard core inside, like a peach stone.

She had thought Sheila would be the opposite of Jonelle, soft underneath her sculpted hair and her blazers and her French manicure. But she is not.

It occurs to her that Sheila is probably her own age, coming up on thirty. Is this reassuring or not?

It has taken Leslie all this time to get a good job, a real job. She can't let anyone else screw it up for her. She has to figure this out, figure out what they want, find her way there.

At any given point, she thinks she knows. Things seem clear. It's only after that she sees she has been misled, or something.

JUNE

When her new nephew, Keegan, is born, she goes over to Mike and Jonelle's with flowers and a gift bag with New Baby! and a pastel print of cartoon animals on it, and a bottle of Crown Royal for Mike, and a Tonka truck for Jackson, because the saleswoman at Toys"R"Us had said: First baby? No? Have you got a gift for the older child, so he won't be jealous? Good up-selling there, and she had fallen for it, because it was definitely more fun to choose a toy truck than little blue sleepers and plush rattles. But when she gets there, Jonelle and the baby are kind of dozy, the baby more like a shrunken human than anything else, like a human raisin, and Jackson at his grandmother's, and her brother Mike busy with a construction project. He says she can hang out and give a hand, though.

Mike's friend Cole, who's also there, says: So, bylaw officer, eh? So what do you do; drive around looking for people watering their lawns on the wrong day?

He's teasing, but as her supervisor, Larry, always says: Ignorance of the law is a great opportunity for education. She says: Municipal bylaws play an important role in maintaining the functioning of the city for the safety and comfort of every city resident. That's directly from the preamble of the hand-book, but she thinks it sums things up precisely.

Yeah? he says. So what are some examples of bylaws?

This is hard to answer, as there are so many. She tries to think of some interesting but not controversial ones. Inline Skates and Skateboards, she says. Bylaw 23-63. To keep activities safe for skaters with respect to traffic and pedestrians. Cemeteries. Bylaw 6-27. To maintain, regulate, and operate cemeteries. Good Neighbour Bylaw 49-1. To promote civic responsibility and encourage good relationships between neighbours.

You got them memorized?

Some, she says. Trying.

They are helping drywall the suite Mike is building in the basement of his new house. Mike has made a run to Rona for more outlet boxes – they had miscounted. Les is holding the panel of drywall in place while Mike's friend Cole attaches it to the studs. She had thought Cole wanted her to hold it up, and had braced herself for the weight, but no – he had a wooden prop called a shoe, weird name, that took the weight, and she has only to press the sheet against the new wall to steady it while Cole drives in a couple of anchor screws.

Do you like it?

The last question whips up in her brain a snarl of disconnected events and issues, so the real answer is not going to work its way up soon. It's okay, she says. Steep learning curve.

What people always say. Then another thought kicks up from the jangle and surfaces.

I'll have full dental when I've been there three months, she says. Yeah. Lot of work to do in there.

Feels the heat rise under her jawbones, then. But Cole seems interested. Right on, he says.

Cole is not a carpenter but knows what he's doing, has a truck and tools. Offered to show Mike the ropes. He's Mike's friend from men's hockey.

Mike never used to play hockey. No money for equipment, when they were kids. Mike's always improving stuff, now.

Mike, her little brother. Now with a wife and two rug rats and a house in a nice neighbourhood. Well. He's making the suite for a mortgage helper. And Jonelle's parents loaned them the down payment. (Grandkids, Mike had said. Best collateral you can have.) But still. How Mike has moved up and up.

Knows which side his bread is buttered on, Gran's voice, twisty as beetle scratchings, says in her head.

You can let go now, Cole says. He's zipping in the drywall screws now with a power drill, *shroom, shroom.* The screws are black, loosely spiraled, with x-shaped slots on their heads. He drives in each new screw in a fluid series of motions, transferring a single one from the row held between the middle fingers of his left hand to his pointer and thumb, his right hand simultaneously swinging the drill up in an arc and connecting with the screw's head, eyeballing it perfectly, the screws, a hand span apart, forming an even line around the perimeter of the drywall sheet and up the middle. As if there were marks there that only he could see.

Like her and Mike's dad. He could do anything well. The rest of them were all cack-handed, though.

You want to do the last couple? Cole asks, holding the drill toward her.

It is heavier than she expected, its blue shell cold and weirdly textured, and it vibrates when she squeezes the trigger. It wobbles all over and the screw goes in completely crooked. Crap. She's useless at it.

Slide the button to reverse it, Cole says. Just take the screw out and try again. She hadn't known that there was a reverse button. Dad never let them touch his tools, of course.

This time he holds the screw to get it started, and she puts two hands on the drill to steady it. Like a girl. It's better, but not perfect. You can tell which one is hers.

Like this, Cole says, and puts his hands on hers, changes the shape of her grip, presses.

The guy-underarm smell, not dirty but foreign. The sense of him too close, biceps, beard.

Her hair swings forward as she hunches, and he scoops it away. Whoa, buddy. Don't want to get your hair too close to a rotating tool. You could lose your scalp.

The chagrin, how close she has come to an accident. She recoils, stumbles awkwardly sideways.

After the incident, they'd put her in a car with a more senior officer, an older guy. That was Larry. He was supposed to give her more orientation.

She has nearly memorized the entire bylaw document. She has always been pretty good at memorizing.

She has tried, riding with Larry, to be more observant, to think things through the way Larry does. Larry will incline his head to something ahead of them in the street, ask: Now, what are we looking for up there? And she'll try to see what he's seeing, to think through things the way he does. And to call it. But she's always wrong. Always.

What are you seeing?

Hedge encroaching on road.

Are you kidding me? It's back six feet. Look again.

Um. Garage under construction? Maybe without permit?

Larry makes a sound like he's clearing something small and scratchy from the roof of his mouth. That's old wood. See the colour? Never got the siding on.

Cyclist without a helmet.

Not our jurisdiction.

What, then?

See that pile of sawdust, there. On the lawn. Tree felling.

No permit?

Yeah, we don't give permits in residential. Need to hire a licensed company. Otherwise, what happens?

What?

First thing, giant freaking branch falls through neighbour's roof, kills Grandma in the bath.

Okay.

That's an image that will help you remember this particular ordinance.

Thanks, she says. She likes Larry. She feels safe with him: She knows where she is. She knows he's going to ride her all day, but that's for her own good.

Only her head full of static, like there's too many signals, too many connections, to put anything together. It's the thought that she might not make it, that she might not meet expectations, that's clouding her mind, of course. But she can't fight through that. It's all around her and inside her, like an invisible gas. It's even part of her, maybe: She feels that it's intertwined with her cells, her brain cells, even. Like it's always been there, latent, silent, but now something has come along and activated it.

It's inside her and part of her and she can't fight it hard enough.

Sometimes the thought comes to her that she might be fired – she might not pass her probationary period. And then it's so bad, it's like air being cut off. Then she can't think at all.

She downloads the manual and sends it to Staples to be printed. Maybe she's not supposed to do that? But if she had a printer at home she could do it and nobody would know, would they? Or is there some sort of thing in the computer that lets people know when you print something off?

She keeps the printout in her kitchen, reads through it while she cooks and eats her breakfast oatmeal and her supper, which is usually some sort of pasta with frozen vegetables boiled in, and a couple of hot dog wieners. Meat is good for you but she doesn't like steak; it hurts her teeth. And chicken. The smell of it raw, and she's had it.

She reads through the printout before bed, falls asleep with it in her hand, sometimes. You'd think she'd dream about the bylaws. But instead she keeps having the dreams where she is the queen, that she's given someone – always some faceless man dressed in black – a command to have someone executed. That's a silly dream, a stupid mixture of *Alice in Wonderland* and her real Gran's album of royal family clippings and her stories about the war.

Mind you, she had been good and scared of Gran. She'd moved in after their mom run off – looked after them and Dad. She didn't take any crap, that was for sure.

Or, maybe more exactly, she made you pay later for any crap. Only you didn't always know at the time that you had done something wrong. Of course, you should have known.

She tells Sheila in HR that she's ready to re-write the general knowledge test. She has already written it – she had to pass it with 73% to get the job in the first place – but one thing that was part of her probation was that she has to write it again.

She gets 98%.

She can stop riding with Larry, Sheila says.

On her way out of the office, Les says, Can I make a suggestion, Sheila? More signs along the walls? Because, half the people that come in here haven't even brought the right forms. They're just wasting their time and ours. They get to the front of the line and they haven't even got a piece of ID with their current address on them.

It's a good idea, and she knows it. She's pumped.

I mean, we shouldn't have to, she says. But between you and I, we're dealing with morons here, aren't we?

That's when Sheila says that she's going to be on a desk job for an unspecified time. And just as the weather is getting really nice.

Mike says: Hell no. It's not a demotion, Lester. You're just getting some on-the-job training. They should have – well, anyway. It'll just get you up the ladder faster.

It's comforting when he calls her Lester, his old nickname for her when they were kids, when she could forget that she had to do the dishes and mop the floor and fold the laundry, because she was the girl, and they could all be brothers together, she and Mike and Paulie and Al Junior. Though it was better to be the girl when Al Junior wanted to beat on her, and Paulie and Mike would stop him.

But better not to be a girl, when Al Junior tried to do those other things, which again Paulie and Mike stopped him.

Mike is going to have two sons. Jackson, the toddler, and the new baby, about to be born, is going to be a boy too. She doesn't know about Paul or Al: hasn't heard from them for years.

Family barbecue is why she's over at Mike's. But it turns out it's Mother's Day. She should have known: Every freakin' holiday, it seems, Mike and Jonelle invite everyone over, or go to Jonelle's family. So Jonelle's parents are here, and her sister with her hubby and kids, and a couple of aunts and cousins – the whole shebang. It's not like Mike's house is that large, either, but he does have a deck and a yard, and the unfinished basement.

And she gets invited to everything, now.

There are too many people, though. She can't really talk to Mike, he's barbecuing, and Jonelle is doing things in the kitchen, though the other adults keep saying, hey, what are you doing? Sit down, put your feet up.

Jonelle looks ready to pop. She's wearing a striped T-shirt dress that hugs her like a sock. Les can't look at her, at the huge curve of her belly, her breasts, but can't look away either.

She's not sure if she's supposed to help watch Jackson or what. There are a lot of adults around, but nobody seems to be controlling the boy. The older kids have gone to the basement – shame on such a nice day – nothing but an old couch and large-screen TV, where the kids are playing with the Wii, down there. Jackson runs back and forth so quickly. The grandmother is sort of looking after him, but there's another baby, and the grandmother is carrying that one around.

Its head is a bit wobbly. It locks glances with her for an instant, over the grandmother's shoulder, like it's going to say something, and a gob of white goo leaps from its mouth and lands on the back of the grandmother's dress.

You've got something.... she says, and the grandmother says, Goodness. Here, can you hold her for a sec while I wipe that off?

The baby's eyes open wide, as if she's been given a maximum fine for something she's going to pretend she knows nothing about. Les holds her carefully a foot away from herself, but in this position her arms start to ache quite quickly.

Oh, there's my milk-pig, one of the cousins says, and scoops the baby out of Leslie's grasp.

Okay. That was kind of abrupt.

She looks around and sees that Jackson has got hold of the

bread knife that someone has left carelessly on the patio table. Accident waiting to happen. She goes after him. What are these people thinking? But nobody's paying attention.

She catches him by the shoulders, says, Give me the knife, please, Jackson.

No, he says.

They're not strict enough with him. She sees that all the time.

She grasps the handle, carefully, mindful of the long, serrated blade, tries to pry his fingers up. Now his face goes red, his eyes bulge, absolutely pig-stupid defiant. He tugs. One of them is going to get a nasty cut.

Give it to me, she says, firmly.

Jackson screams.

She wraps her hands now around his on the handle and squeezes, hard, harder. His face changes. The pitch of his scream changes – the source of the sound moves from his head to his chest. But she feels his fingers loosen, relaxes her hands. The knife clatters to the board floor of the deck.

It has taken only an instant. But now suddenly all the previously oblivious eyes are on her. Conversation chopped off.

Jackson runs to Jonelle, butts his head into her belly, so that Les winces, but Jonelle lifts him to her chest, cuddles him. Jackson's howls and sobs wreaking havoc on the neighbourhood.

All around her, from the vantage of the deck, she can see the rows of houses with their thrusting decks, their flagrant, new-leafed trees, their tall board fences, their glittery, staring windows. Their shining little cars.

When she's moved to the suburban beat of Sedona Hills, on
the hilly south side of the city, she can't believe her luck. To
be out of traffic, to be released from the endless circuit of
writing out parking tickets and clipping them under wipers;
checking complaints of uninsured cars, of noise, of garbage,
which, in the downtown area were usually moves in some
sort of inter-neighbour aggression; of hustling along the street
people and vagabond kids that sprouted palely in the business area and park once the temperatures rose above freezing,
and who were high on something, fresh air at the least, and
verbally or even physically punchy. To be released from the
layers of dust and grit that seemed to blow down from the
surrounding hills all year round and form a tar-like slurry in
the downtown streets and sidewalks.

To be assigned a vehicle! And to shuck the heavy padded
waterproof navy coat, which never fit, too tight in the upper
sleeves, so that her arms stuck out like a penguin's flippers.

She had to buy the uniform out of her salary, a deduction
each paycheque, but she doesn't mind. She wishes she'd had
a uniform all of her life – it saves hard decisions every day.
She likes the beige shirt, crisp as new twenties, and the tan
pants, which are ample, not girly. You're lucky, with your colouring, with your auburn hair, one of the other officers says,
you can wear beige and tan. But she doesn't care about that
appearance stuff – only that she's neat and appropriate, that
she doesn't have to worry anymore about that.

She likes the anonymity, which some of the others complain about. She's not out here to make friends. She wants to do a good job; she wants to help make the city a good place for people to live and do business. But she doesn't need to make friends.

The uniform helps her do her job, which isn't about making people like her.

She's not completely sure what she is supposed to do, though, once she's moved up to the Sedona Hills jurisdiction. Watering days, she knew, and animal control, though that was usually handled by the special branch. Parking, though here there are broad streets and large backyards and she hasn't seen anything yet like a stale-dated license plate, or only on a vintage Mustang up on blocks in a driveway. Some kid rebuilding it maybe. She hadn't been sure if that was an infraction, but when she came back the next week the wheels were off, so moot point.

She's worried about her productivity. If she isn't pulling notices and fines, she's not going to keep this sweet beat – she knows that. Even though Larry, the other officer assigned to this neighbourhood, says, wait a month; things get going in spring. Use your time to familiarize yourself with the layout.

She knows she has to do more than coast, though. If you aren't moving forward, the current is taking you backwards. That's something she read in a book of Mike's, one of many that he's intended to read but probably hasn't. I've skimmed it, he always says. He never liked reading.

Mike's working hard, though. He's two years younger than her, manager at one of the big box electronics stores. When she'd run into him, looking for a computer – well, she knew he worked there, just hadn't seen him in a while – she had been impressed. Good haircut, his skin cleared up, suit jacket and tie. Yup.

Dad would be proud of you, she'd said, and then regretted it, because Mike had made a face, and she'd remembered then that was why they hadn't talked for a few years, their arguments over how they each thought about their father, the arguments that had bubbled out and surprised her, when they had been taking care of their father's stuff, after he had died.

Well, disagreements. Basically, Mike had turned out to have a lot of grudges against their dad, which wasn't fair. Yeah, he was strict. But he'd had to raise four kids after their mother abandoned them. And yeah he drank a little too much, the last few years, but he had lost his job too young for retirement, too old to get another one. And then Gran had died. And Paul and Al Junior had vanished, too – Al was in jail, last she heard, but Paul just never contacted them.

Mike had wanted to rehash everything, to try to find their mother. Get the real story, he said. But that was just stupid. It was over. What their dad had said was true. It had to be.

So she hadn't talked to Mike for five years and then she had gone into that store, maybe to see him, maybe not.

And then almost said the wrong thing. But how was she to know? People were funny. In any instant you could do or say something that seemed okay, and it would turn out that someone nailed you for it. How could anyone ever know?

So she had accidentally-on-purpose bumped into Mike again, and he had invited her over, to meet his wife, his son. So, okay. An agreement to disagree, they'd had to settle for that. Because Mike was still bitter: He wanted to sit in the evenings with a beer and talk about how Dad had beat on them and how Gran had ratted them out all the time, knowing Dad would beat the crap out of them. Even though she gave them lots of affection, did the extras like buying them the clothes they wanted, not just the cheapest, and baking cookies and birthday cakes.

Of course, you didn't get beat on so much, Mike had said one night, because you were the girl. That's when she had said: We will have to agree to disagree, Mike. Because her blood just boiled when he said that crap.

Anyway, it's nice to go to Mike's, to have family. Their dad never got to see grandkids. In some way, maybe, she's doing it for him.

Mike is all about rising in his work, which of course he should. And about improving himself, improving his life. Which is good, but he should read those books. They're really interesting: They make you see that if you don't work the hardest, be the strongest, you'll get beaten down. That's just the way it is. It's nature.

She needs to work harder. To figure out her new neighbourhood, to figure out how, in these clean open streets, she can make her work stand out.

There it is on the map she studies every evening, the little squiggle that is the lane, dangling from the adjoining street like a loose thread. She has never driven down it, though she has passed the opening a few times, off the side street. On the map she can see that it's backed by the kinds of houses with complex, spreading roof structures, and pools.

She can see, too, on the map, thanks to those Google photographs, what the lane contains: parked cars. And that's a problem. She knows very well, from her previous assignment, that there is no parking in lanes. Fire trucks and ambulances can't get through if there's parking. And that's what parking bylaws are all about: access.

So someone, Larry maybe, or her predecessor, didn't notice, or turned a blind eye. But a rule is a rule.

She'll go on a Saturday, on her own time. She'll take an extra booklet with her, because on a Saturday, she knows this from visiting Mike in his neighbourhood, there are going to be a shitload of cars.

She's going to make a splash, this week.

She parks her vehicle in the lane, but has to walk along Calvin Street, which has no parking, to approach each residence's front door.

Twenty-three houses. None with a garage in front, or a driveway. Because there is no access from the street, due to some anomaly in the construction of this subdivision. Twenty-three houses, along this stretch of Calvin Street, where the back lane access is the only parking available to the residents. Twenty-three houses that are obviously exempt from the bylaw prohibiting parking in alleyways and access lanes. Of which the residents are very aware. And that is why the twenty-three tickets resulted in a shit-storm of angry phone calls and drop-ins.

She pressed her uniform the night before, though it's made of some resilient fibre that pretty well conforms to its original shape even after being pummelled in a top-loading washer.

She takes along the stack of letters in their municipal letter-head envelopes. They are all the same, addressed to Dear Homeowner, printed out multiply, signed individually. They all contain the apology, which Sheila in HR helped her write.

She had thought they would be mailed. But no.

She parks her car – her own car, not the city vehicle – in the lane. She walks to the upper end of the pertinent section of Calvin Street. She walks up the first set of steps. Rings the doorbell. Waits.

Her collar is tight and abrasive under her chin. Focus on that. Not the constriction in her chest, the wobbly feeling in her knees, like their hydraulics have been broached. Not the sensation that a plug has been pulled in her gut.

The sky is the colour of an empty blue bowl, and the bushes and trees almost purple, swollen with the expectation of leaf. She tries again.

THE FL WERS
F THE DRY
INTERI R

IN LATE MAY THE LIGHT IS JUST RIGHT: the sun a little to the
north, the ceiling high and clear, still, tempered by moisture
in the air. A cool bluish light. In the morning, as she walks,
the shadows fall to the southwest, purple, velvet-textured.

She walks across rangeland, high above the river. The hills
here are folded and scoured by wind. They are like stiff bat-
ter: time their cook. Only the north-facing gullies support
trees. The path she walks along is an old cattle path. It winds
through her property and the next and next. She follows it,
ignores the Private Property signs, bends and straddles to
pass through where the barbed wire is stretched by decades
of opening to admit foot travellers. (One of her cousins owns
this land: He does not mind her crossing it, she thinks.)

The dog lollops ahead of or behind her, scooting under the barbed wire, leaving tufts of buff hair for the songbird's nests. Mourning cloak butterflies, scattered like fall leaves along the shaded sections of the path, sipping the dew that has not yet evaporated, drinking the soil's moisture, now rise, fluttering weakly when she disturbs them.

She's a ground-watcher, a noter of what is at the feet. Her landmarks are horizontal: deadfalls, a large granite egg, half-buried in the earth. (The granite egg of sufficient size that a woman could be curled up inside, ready to hatch.) The flora: pasture sage, rabbit brush, antelope bush.

It's the season of yellow and creamy flowers, along the path. Wishy-washy colours, she has always thought. Insipid. Cinquefoil and wild strawberries, now, where the ground is boggy, decorated with cow pats. Milk vetch, Thompson's paintbrush, the pale cousin of the plant they used to call Indian paintbrush. Lemonweed. Alumroot, an astringent bitter herb her grandmother ground up and used to treat cancer. It didn't work. Curious that the notion seems to persist: Root out the cancer with dreadful poisons. The nastier, the more efficacious. Near a stand of aspens, a glade of false Solomon's seal. She's never been able to discover which is false: the Solomon, or the seal, or the plant.

Field locoweed, poisoner of cattle. Death camas, little cones of delicate starry cream-coloured blooms.

An anthill, heaped segments of pine needle, black and burnt umber, and when she looks closer, the ants themselves, the black abdomen and rusty-orange thorax and head, moving on the surface. The anthill alive. If she were to give it a poke with her walking stick, they'd all boil out, smelling acrid, metallic. Formic acid. As a child, she had believed that if you buried a dead bird in an anthill, the ants would strip it to the bone. You'd have a nice bird skeleton. Had her cousins told her that?

The Saskatoon bushes, beaded with hard green berries, unripe. From a tall bush, warning chirps, and she sees the hummingbird, perched, then darting past her, swoops so quick she can't follow it. A buzz, a whir, at her eye, her ear. It's a routine: This fellow attacks her in this spot every time she comes by. He's comic, a miniature Messerschmitt. Comedy located in scale. Tragedy, too. The size or duration of something, but always in proportion to something else. Our expectations. Our sense of the construction of the world. A child's sense of a year. Her dog's lifespan. Hers. The age of the trees, the soil, the hills. The infinite. Beginnings are not recognizable as beginnings, except afterward. Endings not recognized before they arrive.

IN EARLY APRIL she begins to make this walk, when the ice has thawed from the deer paths, the snow has retreated to pockets on the north cheeks of boulders and slopes. Winter clings at this elevation, three thousand feet. Then the metallic glint of buttercups among the desiccated grass, the funeral-bouquet scent of the mission bells. The sky washed, threaded with the *scree, scree* of kestrels. The exposed granite and limestone shelves, lichen feeding on raw stone.

Everything new to the dog, in its second spring.

She didn't remember later whether she had tripped over

a root or vine or whether the machinery of her brain had hiccupped, short-circuited its gyroscope function. She had left the main path because the dog had left her: something else – chipmunk, marmot, grouse – pulling him away. The one drawing the other, all connected, a chain. Then the disconnect, herself suddenly prone, several feet lower than the path, head lower than her heels. Her hands had met some rocky edge and her palms were torn open, burning and throbbing. Iron taste of blood.

She had fallen partway into a large old rosebush, which had broken her fall. She heard her clothes tear as she extricated herself on hands and knees. Back down the path, the dog appearing suddenly at her heel: He'd missed the whole thing. One knee not right: a catch, a dislocation, that sent her limping.

On the road she had met her cousin Sim in his pickup truck. He had braked too suddenly, the flattening of shock on his face through the open window. Holy moly, Lilah. What'd you do?

In his truck cab, sliding looks across at her. She'd felt fine, except for the stinging in her palms. Her knee quiet now, the weight off of it. But he wouldn't drop her at her house.

Only in the emergency waiting room washroom, glancing into the mirror, she'd finally understood. Blood had poured from some gash on her head and dried and blacked out half her face. She looked like she'd been half-peeled.

That had been one beginning.

SHE CALLS THE DOG, walks on. Now, the frondy stands of the asparagus, the stalks that she hadn't picked in April but allowed to grow. The finest fern. She's tried to transplant it to her garden, both root and red berry, but it won't take: It likes only this old pasture land, this thin sandy patch here along the old fence line. Wild and not-wild. In April, she finds the clumps, snaps off the pinkish-green stalks, puts them into a plastic bag kept in her pocket for that purpose. If there are enough, steams off the bitterness, steams them till they're just crunchy, concocts a saucepan of hollandaise and eats a platter of them. Spring greed: They must be full of vitamins her body is craving.

When she forages, she does so greedily. She'll gobble whole handfuls of blue-black Saskatoon berries, spitting out the seeds; she'll pluck handfuls of rosehips, nibble off the apple-flavoured red skins, drop cottony innards and seeds into the tall grass. She feels her cells imbibe. Something potent enters her, the green force of the rangeland. The molecules inside her now, the atoms of this place, after so many decades.

How many decades? Seven, since her mother had dropped her here, dropped her, half-grown, as people from the city drive out this road their no-longer-manageable half-grown dogs and cats and leave them to starve or be eaten by coyotes. Dropped her with her grandparents, though, to grow up with cousins and second cousins on ancestral ranchland.

The Allingham-Coogans, the largest ranching family in the region. English squires and Irish horse thieves, her mother had always said.

The molecules insinuated into her genes, even. Is that possible? She has seen on television that the carbons in fish mark their feeding grounds.

Down the slope, now, some slippery blue clay and raw-edged shale; down to the pond, held in the hill's hollow like a secret. The pond is full; there's runoff, there's the underground spring, the one the feeds the aspens, the damp ground where the Solomon's seal grows. The pond is unexpected, when you come across it; although it can be heard a long way off, the calls of blackbirds carving up the air: the klaxon shrieks, the liquid warble. In the tangles of dried reeds around the perimeter, rustlings and strange croaking or quacking. Like coming upon an invisible city.

The dog bounds off, and she calls him back, sharply: There are nests, hatchlings. Now, swimming toward them, the chick of a mud hen, the naked red head like a shameful body part. It's alone, keeps up a sharp peeping as it continues its circle of the pond. She doesn't see adults, feels a stab of worry: Left on its own, it's a quick meal for a crow or coyote. But a threesome of rusty-headed, blue-billed goldeneye chug along in the chick's wake, slowing when it slows, changing direction as it tacks. Are they guarding it? Keeping an eye out for it? Doesn't seem plausible. Where are the parents? Why don't they come out, answer that plaintive peeping, chivvy their offspring back to the safety of the group?

She wishes she had not seen the chick alone, its blood-coloured bald head, its peeping.

She turns, urges the dog to heel. The parent birds are likely hiding with the rest of the brood, waiting for the danger to pass. They'll sacrifice one chick for the rest. Will that lone chick, breaker of protocol, iconoclast, survive to pass on its genes? The mud hens are not rare, as waterfowl go.

The dog looks back at the pond, looks at her, gives a small whine. He's thirsty, or he thinks the chick is fair game, easy pickings. *No*, she says. He's a young dog; she's still training him. Part border collie, part Alsatian: he has a long muzzle, soft ears, a striking coat of black and white and tan. She wants the impossible from him: to know when to take the initiative, when to submit. She has achieved this fine-tuned behaviour with his predecessors; she lets him know that she considers him capable of developing a more intuitive set of responses, too.

He heels with only the subtlest show of reluctance. He will work out, she thinks.

At the place where the trail crosses the dirt road, a pickup truck approaches, half-ton, dusty green. Her cousin Sim's daughter, Donna. She waits, and Donna slows, pauses the truck. Her dog, a cousin to this one, jumps around in the bed, barks a greeting. Donna ignores him. She's a big woman, beefy forearm out the window, man's T-shirt, red hair dusted with grey. In her forties now. It was clear when she was nine or ten she'd be the one to take on the farm.

Goin' to town, she says. Need anything?

No. Not today.

Donna nods, releases the clutch; the truck moves on.

They are keeping an eye on her. They don't like her to walk out alone. But everybody walks out alone.

She has told Sim that she is training the dog, that it will learn to go for help. This is only half true.

HER DAUGHTER MERCEDES on the telephone asks, Are you painting?

Yes, she says, briefly. She doesn't mention the yellow-ivory of the morning, the daubing she's been doing since. Pale yellow-creams; how to put those on the canvas, fine, but then to convey that other sense. What it is, that's the problem. Bitter alumroot, locoweed, cinquefoil flat like woodcuts, starry death-camas. Death or life? How are cream, pale yellow, dead? Bone, ivory, waxy pallor. But bone isn't bone: Here on the rangeland it's blue-grey, fissured, lichened – bone of cattle becoming stone. Maybe that's it, the complement. But she's over-thinking it; she hasn't done it right, yet: hasn't sucked it up into her bones, her marrow, the places she works from.

Getting ready for the show? Mercedes asks.

Maybe, she says. Drags herself inside from a great distance. How Mercedes in her adolescent years shouted at her: You are not a supportive mother. Her mind edging out the side door, suddenly Not Home, surprising even herself. Now Mercedes just waits. What goes on in her head?

How's the knee? Mercedes asks.

It's been sore, the rain. Nothing too bad, though. (It's her hands that pain her, though she does not mention this. Why not?)

Are you taking the glucosamine?

It's a health call then. Mercedes giving her the checkup by phone. But no: Mercedes asks, now: Did you get the toilet fixed?

She has to think back for that one, a couple of weeks ago, but yes: trip to the hardware store; replaced the handle. Everyday thing, just happened to mention it once. Not health, then: general check-in. Her daughter's mind moving through her house, the fact of her body, remotely, robot investigator, those spider-spies in the movie she saw a few years back. Prying open the eyelid. Discovering the intention, crimes not yet committed. Perhaps that's what Mercedes is looking for. She will need to be cautious. But Mercedes has moved on, now, her voice changing timbre.

So, she says.

Now is it going to be an announcement or request? Either fork leads to the minefields. She makes herself go still, listens to the suddenly stiff leather bag of her lungs. Expand, contract. Expand.

After fifty years, still this clumsy dance. But still speaking: She ought to be grateful for that, she supposes. She has a vision now of Mercedes leaving for school, her pleated skirt blooming stiffly around her thighs, her hair, oak-coloured, bound in braids, sun picking out the golds and reds, her lifted chin: *Goodbye, Mother Dear.* At five already a fortress, a small tower, cloistered, self-sufficient. Herself dressed in similar stiffness, tailored slacks, fitted shirt, beehive hair. Waiting for the child to round the corner, to be out of sight, waiting to return to the washing of her matched dinnerware, the ironing of jeans and socks, the carefully plotted world with its clear clean rules, where her mind could float safely, tethered.

Mercedes in her teens, the lights of her bedroom on at two in the morning. What woke her to that? A sound, maybe. Her daughter's sallow face, hair scraped back painfully, the hairline and chin angry with pustules and scabby sores, looking up from her textbooks.

I'm *okay*, Mother.

Her colleagues had talked about their adolescent children in terms of drugs, dropping out, running away. Her daughter in her high room, its small window, disciplining herself, making straight As, the yearly awards, valedictorian, the scholarship, the dean's list. She had been, so clearly, *okay*. Herself in school then, too, painfully disciplining her hand, her eye; finding the doorway into her own thoughts.

Mercedes venturing her inner life, asking for a favour, so rarely, and always awkwardly. She herself always means to be more open, more generous, but is never prepared. Both of them stiff, ungracious. She always says the wrong thing: She knows that. But her daughter obscures, misdirects: not in a cloud of vagueness – she's used to that, she knows lots of artists who do that – but somehow in the middle of sounding focused and business-like and pragmatic.

She's always caught off guard; she's always lured down the wrong pathway, in these conversations with Mercedes: always ambushed. You don't understand.

Mercedes says, *So*, and she says, *Yes*, warily, and knows that she's already taken the step in the wrong direction, is already, somehow, doomed.

She has been standing in the kitchen, but remembers that the phone is cordless, strolls to the sun porch, settles herself in the old armchair, first lifting the cat out of the seat. Cat hair but she has on old clothes, it doesn't matter. The porch is east-facing, catches the morning sun, as a porch should. The house she had designed to her own specifications: the right proportion of rooms, of windows; the right alignment for light. Light for waking, for gardening, for painting. Walls to block the plateau wind. The house fits her needs. She gathers it around herself, carapace, prepares herself to be found wanting.

She's at her daughter's mercy now. Who had told her? Judith. Now the phone calls come regularly, the intrusions, the attempts to dislodge her.

She has tried to be canny. Her upcoming show has proved a good excuse – a decoy. She has some more work to do for it. She needs the studio.

Mercedes had argued about weakness and falling and danger and worry, about causing others distress. She had answered: I don't want to move. How quavery her voice had been that day. But it suited her, now, to have it sound so.

Her pause, her huge sigh. Finding some old truculence to dress it up, like pickles from the root cellar shelf. Not too much. Don't overdo. If I must, I must, she had said. Then, and this was crucial: I need a couple of months. To sort papers. To get ready for the show. To find a home for the dog. (A genuine raw spot, when she thought of the dog.)

It had worked. She is good at this. She should have made an effort to learn it much earlier in her life.

Now she must pay for her three months' grace with Mercedes' regular check-ins. But that is a condition she can cope with.

I KNOW ALL ABOUT YOU, Hal had said.

And: I could fit you in my cupped hands. Putting out his hands to show, long as her feet. He was all long bones and angles, Hal. Like a folding yardstick. A jackknife.

He was like anything made to compact itself and pretend not to take up its proper amount of space. Collapsible chairs, tent trailers, Murphy beds. What was it she had seen the other week in Canadian Tire? Collapsible silicone colanders, for straining vegetables. The colours had appealed to her: turquoise, coral, moss green. She wanted one of each. But the idea of it being flat, popping out. Collapsible things catch and pinch the fingers, in the folding. And they are mean, ungenerous objects. Intended to be frugal, what they do is cheat, try to squeeze more into a space than is justified. They don't want to pay for the space they take up. They want something for nothing.

Hal, renting a U-Haul whenever they moved: always a size too small. Then wanting to leave things behind, not to make a second trip across town. Her things, mostly. Things she valued. You don't want that, pointing to her grandmother's chair, her easel, a table she used for potting plants. What she had left behind: collections of shells, doll furniture, boxes of fabric scraps she intended for making magnificently textured and coloured wall hangings. Her mother's Limoges plaques, Stations of the Cross, not that she cared so much for them, but they had been her mother's. Books and books and books.

He did not want her to take up space.

Why had she agreed? (She'd learned not to agree; she'd argued, for some of it.) She had tried to make herself fit. She'd jettisoned pieces of herself, left them behind.

There, there. What does it matter, now? What would she want back, now, that she hasn't been able to replace? Or couldn't replace, if she wanted?

Her shoes, maybe. She'd had a fabulous collection, vintage. Whenever she was in a new city: off to the second-hand stores, the Anglican rummage sales, the flea markets. (Such disparaging names, but she remembers these places always as being housed in places of high architecture, dim halls with arches and buttresses, coffered ceilings, thickly carved moldings. Halls of the dim past, layered with the dust of a more munificent time. Treasure halls.) And for her collection of shoes, with a size five foot, she'd been able to pick up gems, hand-tooled leather, colours of pre-Raphaelite paintings, often nearly unworn, still in their original boxes. You can't find shoes like that anymore. Not here.

And the one thing that had come back to her: her grandmother's chair, the armchair in her sun porch. But that's another story.

Hal said: I want to put you on a watch fob. I want to wear you on a chain. I want to keep you in a little gilt birdcage.

She had thought he meant her size. He was a foot taller than she was. She had not been paying enough attention.

She had pushed the buggy with the second baby, Tommy, to the school in the mornings and again in the afternoons. You did this when your children were very small, but not later. She had learned the rules. She had cut her hair like the other women and worn clothes like theirs, pedal pushers from April to October, pleated trousers from October to March, with fitted blouses and jackets. The T-shirt had not been invented, except for little boys and labouring men, and jeans were called dungarees and not permitted at school. There were some women, some of the mothers, for that was their context of their coming together, who wore longish tweedy skirts and braids pinned to their heads. There were women, especially a couple of years later, when her second child started school, who wore their hair long and ironed flat, and skirts halfway up their thighs. These women it was important to stand back from, to ignore.

This all taught her by Hal. She had allowed it. Had wanted to leave behind the ranch, to fit into another world.

When her chance at freedom had come, she had not been careful or kind. Had not been prescient.

SIM DROPS BY with his grandson Corey: They will install her new automatic gate. The old gate has a motor, but it's a Rube Goldbergian contraption she built herself: a garage door opener with a pulley mounted on a tall post, the swing gate not functioning in deep snow or wind, both of which are plentiful up in these hills.

Sim is often helpful.

Her mother had left her this piece of land that she was supposed to sell back to her cousins – it had been carved out of the main ranch – but she did not. It had a good building site, a stream, a stand of fir. She had built a house on it, commuted into town to teach for ten years, until she retired. It should be Sim's land, but he is gracious, and helpful.

Sim unbolts and drags away the old gate. Corey is not helpful. He is a big boy, but mentally handicapped. He capers, chatters, asks questions, but can't seem to see where he could lend a hand. Even the simplest effort. She sees that Sim has brought him along not as a helper, but to give Judith some space, to get Corey out from underfoot for the morning.

Corey is the son of Sim's son Ken, who married a cousin. That is supposed to be a bad thing.

Now Sim is digging out the old pulley post, fifteen feet high, with a crossbeam near the top, like a gibbet, she thinks. He digs out its foundation. She calls Corey and the dog to come stand by her while Sim pushes the post over.

She had put it in herself. How? She walks over, tries to hoist the post with its crossbar, out of curiosity, but Sim rushes to her, lifts it onto his own shoulder, drags it toward the truck. She watches him walk toward the truck, the post with its crossbar bending him over.

Sim is a decade younger than she, still in young, hale old age.

She grew up with him, but it is still great kindness he shows her. He is her second cousin. And also, she suspects, her half-brother. His hand on Corey's shoulder, the gentleness. They are a family that does not touch. She does not think Sim has ever touched her, except to hand her down from his truck at the hospital. But then even her children do not touch her.

THE NURSE AT THE EMERGENCY ROOM: Veronika. She was very young, her skin over her snowplow cheekbones and around her eyes taut and fine-pored and dewy: rose-petal. Accented English. She had moved unhurriedly, ceremonially, had made her preparations, arranged the little packages on the tray, the graceful swoop of her fingers, the cupping of her hands as she aligned the objects revealing a deep slow pleasure in the activity. She had drawn up and sat on a stool, her knees pressing up against Lilah's, had pulled on gloves that were thin and supple as the sloughed skin of salamanders, had taken Lilah's chin between her left thumb and forefinger as if handling porcelain. Slowly, ceremoniously, she had opened packet after packet of gauze, dabbed. The dabbing had stung, but lightly, like small shocks. It had come away burnt sienna, carmine, rose-madder. Lilah was being painted. She was the canvas.

Veronika had dabbed and dabbed, lightly, delicately. She used the corners of the gauze to take out grit; she leaned forward, her eyes wide and intent, her lips soft, parted.

She cleaned Lilah's face, then her gouged palms. She brushed on ointment; she pressed to Lilah's skin, with her fine translucent fingertips, the adhesive wings of butterfly bandages. She took Lilah's blood pressure again, her fingers moving in a graceful wave pattern even as she squeezed the bulb, as she listened through her stethoscope. The diaphragm of the stethoscope was a gold coin pressed to Lilah's arm, for luck.

Even gathering the stained gauze pads together to drop them into the waste bag, her fingers moved reverently.

HER SON TOM CALLS HER on Skype.

Where are you now? she asks.

Nepal.

She never knows. He has called from Botswana, Laos, Peru. And once from Vancouver, only an hour's flight away. He had zipped back to renew his passport, wasn't staying, wouldn't see her.

The video feed isn't working well; she gets only frozen, pixelated aspects of his face.

The last time he had visited, he had been jet-lagged, had slept through the first two days of a three-day stay. She had left him alone, but at last had crept into the room to look at him, and had seen how, in his sleep, the flesh slipped from the side of his face, hung from the bones, as if it were melted wax. She had tiptoed out. Wished she had not seen that. His youth gone.

He asks how she is so casually that she might think he hadn't heard, if she didn't know him so well. She wants to say, come home to me, my son, but that is not a language either of them speaks.

He says, Maybe they've made a mistake. You seem pretty lively.

Oh, I am well, she says.

Still painting? he asks.

Well, you know, she says.

He says he will fly her to Kathmandu. She can go for guided hikes in the Himalayas. She can paint the famous rhododendrons. She believes, while he is speaking, that she will do this. That is Tommy's gift: He travels the world selling belief – in himself, in possibility.

When he was a boy, when they were driving somewhere, he would sometimes say, urgently, putting his hand on her arm: Dad can't speak to you like he does. I will make him stop. And once: Mom. We should move out. She had, at those points, felt it possible.

In eleventh grade, the first day, he'd come for supper laughing. He'd said that he had gone to school, was standing in the schoolyard with his friends waiting for the bell to ring, the doors to open, and it had occurred to him that he was now sixteen years old, and not legally obligated to be in school, and he had laughed and walked out of the school grounds, walked downtown and got himself a job.

He would please himself from now on, he said. If they didn't like it, he'd move out.

Hal didn't like it. She had not interfered. She had let Tom go.

She had been so in the throes of her own need to escape that she had barely lifted her head to wish Tom well.

He'll come back in September, he says. He'll come back for her show.

Yes, she says. That will be lovely.

She wants to see him, now, with the ache of roots for underground water. She peers at the screen, but the pixelated image disintegrates, and there is only grey.

If she said: Come sooner, come in the summer. But she must not. If she does, she'll give herself away, she'll lose her plan. She must let go of him now.

SHE TOO HAD ESCAPED, but not with Tommy's éclat or poise. She had made a mess.

When the college had opened, in the early seventies, she had enrolled. Hal hadn't wanted her to. She'd thought it was because he lacked imagination, but really it was that he knew too much: He had foreseen what would happen, that she would find there her exit. That the more she learned, the more she would outgrow the pocket he reserved for her.

In painting class, her instructor had said: Don't be afraid to make a mess, and she had made a mess. She doesn't approve of this kind of leaving, though she understands now that it is sometimes all that can be imagined. It is the only landscape into which women can conceive of disappearing, sometimes: the only one they know.

It is better than chewing off one's own hind foot.

ON HER WALKS SHE GATHERS FLOWERS to dissect and paint. On the canvas, blown up hundreds of times, they become something else: a trick of scale. The something else from her own perception, her mind, her life.

Here is the locoweed blossom, now: its downy sheath, its lobes and clefts, its colour of clotted cream, its scent of butter. She uses the magnifying glass; she sees the petals pursed like closed fingers, the pistil like a periscope with eyelashes. One doubled petal has dark green eye spots, but they can't be seen unless the flower is pulled apart. A flower that secretly watches. The field pussytoes, dry as paper. Each toe a mass of tiny flowers, so small they can't be made out without the magnifying glass. What is hidden, unsuspected. Each petal the size of a split second. Each stamen like a nerve ending, a neural thread.

The pussytoes, her field guide says, can produce seeds without fertilization. Each daughter plant will be genetically identical to the mother.

DOLORES, HER MOTHER, never had said who Lilah's father was. One of her cousins had said to Lilah, after she'd come back to live on the ranch, when, as teens, they'd ride up to one of the lakes, brave the leeches and cold to swim and lie on the baked, cattle-churned mud, smoking and trading sexual information: You were always supposed to be the child of immaculate conception. She'd understood it was the adults joking. She'd already noticed that she looked exactly like photographs of her mother, in the photos of Dolores as a child. Not a little like, but exactly.

She'd believed that she had sprung from Dolores spontaneously, as Athena from the head of Zeus. Only once, at a family gathering – her grandfather's funeral, likely – that had brought Dolores back to Canada, back to the ranch, she'd seen the bodily ease between Dolores and Sim's father, Dolores' first cousin, Derek. She'd been old enough to see it: the way they aligned, walking, talking, sitting, as if they were two halves of something. Her grandmother had said, those two were always thick as thieves, but Betty, Derek's scrappy Liverpudlian war bride, had smoldered, then found occasion to attack Dolores. There had been scratching, hair-pulling. It was clear that the interaction between Dolores and Derek caused Betty some misery, at any rate.

Of her first years Lilah can only remember always rushing to catch trains. When she was older, Dolores, visiting, would say: Don't you remember that funny man in the Champs-Élysées, or, that café in Madrid, or Trieste? Things like that. And Lilah didn't, though perhaps this was willfulness. When the war had broken out, Dolores had taken her to Scotland for a couple of years – there they had lived in a castle. She doesn't remember this. She imagines, because it is necessary, that Dolores fought to give birth to her, to keep her, to keep her safe. After she'd been deposited at her grandparents', Dolores had joined the Wrens, gone back to Europe. Lilah had met her only as a stranger, then: Delores a glittery, glamorous woman, out of place on the ranch, in Canada, with her French magazines, her whiskey, her cigarillos, her scorn for anything conventional. (Always, in Lilah's memory, wearing a green velvet turban pinned with an amethyst orchid-shaped brooch, though that can't be accurate.)

Dolores had not kept her wicked insouciance to the end, but, as she had floundered from surgery to surgery, had become increasingly bitter. She'd had parts of her lungs removed three times; then of her stomach and bowel, and her toes. Her vision had failed, then her kidneys. Her heart had kept working, though: She had lived years, in what must have been constant pain.

You wouldn't let a dog suffer like this, she's said to Lilah, or to the caregivers the family had employed, when she'd moved back to Canada, not to the ranch but to the town. You'd shoot it. You wouldn't let it linger in agony.

At Dolores' funeral, Mercedes, who had nursed her, said she was a grand old lady with endless spirit, and Tommy said that she'd given him a shot of whiskey every time he visited, from the time he was eleven. Lilah herself had not spoken at her mother's funeral, but had thought, at last, to admire Dolores' core selfishness. She was not a good citizen. She was as natural as coyote scat, full of hair and small bones. That was something better, perhaps.

Not sprung from the head of Dolores, but from the land itself, the rangeland cared for by six generations of her family. The Allinghams, English squires, and the Coogans, cattle rustlers and train robbers. One Coogan ancestor had married a Secwépemc woman, so they had even that longer claim to the land.

MACHINES AND WIRES to eavesdrop on her heart. Her doctor draws up a chair, shows her a printout: the confessions of her secret valves and chambers. What do they tell him, those lines of seismography?

You're fine, the doctor says. You have the heart of a healthy fifty-year-old.

Is this a good thing? Does she want this? A high-performance motor in an aging body – is that supposed to be a good thing?

Days later, stripped and inserted into a thick-walled cylinder, like a deep-sea submersible. Beeps and lights: She must hold perfectly still. She is under investigation now: her brain being sliced into leaves, to be read like a book, not for pleasure, but critically.

This new doctor, the specialist, is South African, and named Dr. Pontius. He shows her the image of the scans on his computer screen. There it is, the evidence, the shadow at the core of her brain, the unwelcome guest, the interloper. Her secret sharer. It cannot be extracted, he says, and she believes him. It blooms darkly, in its crevice, but will not spring from her head, will not be set free.

The brain is a little swollen, he says. There is pressure on certain areas. Lack of balance, he says. Possible blackouts. In the future, loss of motor control. Of vision. Significant impairment. He'll give her steroids for the swelling and send her to a radiologist. The radiologist will use lasers to line things up precisely, and will shoot at the thing with invisible waves that will damage its cells, cause it to shrink. Though likely not to disappear.

He says she must not drive anymore and she has to call Sim to drive into town, and have Judith drive her and her station wagon home. Her fall in April, he says: temporary blackout. She can expect more.

SO APRIL WAS THE BEGINNING. April, the season of the massive, showy balsamroot, with its large fleshy cottony grey leaves (like old women's underpants, she thinks), the tiny peacock flower and fringe cups with their thread-like stems, their exquisite petals, The vast difference in scale. For the specialist, it is a matter of problem solving, not personal tragedy. She appreciates that. It's the way you look at it. Painters in the nineteenth century had considered landscape depictions flawed if they lacked a human figure.

It was Judith who called Mercedes, of course. It was a betrayal, but only because it went against Lilah's wishes. From anyone else's point of view, simply necessity.

NOW EARLY JUNE: paintbrush and penstemon: the figwort family. Lupins and vetches: pea family. Shiny buttercup-like cinquefoil and wild strawberries and feathery avens: the rose family. The wild rose in bloom. The deep, flagrant, fragrant pink. The rose scent. The whole open rolling plateau fragrant with rose. She walks, with the dog. She is training the dog, but not as a war-zone medic. She is training him to run home and wait. This is not easy: It is not in his nature.

She lies in the bracken that grows where the stream runs underground. With her stick she lowers herself onto her knees, and then to her belly, curls her legs. Go, Peter, she says. He whines. She gives him a small treat, a piece of liver. When he runs home to his kennel, he will find another piece. And he will trigger the new gate closed, so he can't come back. It is taking a long time to teach him this. She has had to give the signal, then walk him back, many times.

She is training him to abandon her.

This is her second dog. She hadn't wanted any dog, had resisted the first for many years, but Sim had said she needed one if she were to live alone at her age, and Donna had given her one of her pups, a border collie bitch. The dog had grown on Lilah. She had come to see her as a companion, to feel her feelings. When she was four years old, the dog had got into some coyote bait – she guessed it was that, though the stuff was illegal – and had become violently ill, writhing and crying and shitting. She'd called Sim to help her get the dog to the vet, but he'd been away, he and his wife Judith, on holiday. Donna hadn't been home either. She hadn't known any of her neighbours. The dog had writhed and cried. When she tried to bring her water, she had snapped at her, and she'd thought: rabies.

She'd wanted to kill it, then, to put it out of its misery. Had called animal control but they couldn't get anyone out till after the weekend.

She'd tried Donna again but she still wasn't home. She wanted someone with a gun.

She'd got it into her head that she could hang it. How? Thick gloves, rope, pulley. But she hadn't been able to noose it: The dog had fought her attempts, though she'd kept up a low desperate pleading. Then she'd thought: blow to the head. But she'd been afraid that she couldn't hit hard enough, small as she was: would only cause more suffering. Drowning. Asphyxiation. These were too slow.

The bitterness of being helpless in the face of suffering. She'd put the radio on loud to cover the crying, stayed in the house, the dog on the porch. Donna, back finally, had brought a rifle.

A person ought to be able to stop the suffering of something they care for. Someone.

She had not wanted another dog, but now he will be necessary. He will abandon her, as taught. Then, when it is time, he will lead them back. Sim and Donna, it will be, she guesses. A hard thing for them but they are part of this land; they will not be shocked.

The purples and blues of the lupine, the penstemon, the wild delphinium they call monk's hood, or aconite, the mariposa lily. The blooms in their glory as complex and original and exquisite as any cultivar. She is gathering the last, now: She has already planned out these paintings; she could finish them with no more harvesting, but it is an excuse to go out, to continue with the dog's conditioning.

She walks back along the cattle tracks, employing her stick. Her house in the distance now, its blue metal roof a dried petal of sky.

To give herself up to the flowers, to the day. To know each day as unique, one in a procession. To claim one's space in the day, the landscape: no more or less. To do the necessary.

Here is Mercedes, now, waiting in her driveway, foiled by the new gate. Waiting by her car. Mercedes frowns: You're walking without the dog?

The dog is lying in his house, as she has taught him, waiting quietly. Good dog, she thinks at him. He thumps his tail against the ground.

He chases the ground-nesting chicks, she says. Mercedes has never driven up without telephoning, before. She'll have to be careful. Double back, throw her off the trail. Distract her. Ask her for something, perhaps, that she'll disapprove of. Put her off the scent.

To be prepared. To outwit, if outrunning is impossible. To nose out the hiding places. To have a back door, a secret exit, an escape hatch. To use subterfuge, to be alert, to have ears and eyes and nose tuned to the special frequencies of opportunity and the enemy's stealth.

Tommy too. He'll call again, he'll propose a visit. He'll decide to bestir himself early from Kathmandu. She'll need to divert him: to give him an alternate story, to make him want to believe it, to look away.

Winter would have been better, but they won't give her until winter. August will be fine, too: the sun for warmth, the land then at its most arid. She has what she needs. Between her mother and her new friends the doctors, she has what she needs.

To leave herself free recourse. To let her follow her nature. To walk surely toward the edge of the day; to let her cells pull shut the gates, not aimlessly tick down their last usefulness. To dissolve into purest matter, the stuff of infinity: calcium carbon nitrogen, those sparkling potent atoms. To return to the most minute, and to the infinite. To return to the dry hills what is theirs.

She unlocks the gate. She waits for Mercedes to drive through and park and get out of the car, and says: Come inside, now. We'll have some tea. She moves toward her house, her pleasing house. It is still standing.

Mercedes will curse her: will send her off with a curse. And then she will let her go. She will make it as easy as she can: She has taken care of the paperwork, and she will say what has to be said. But that is not now; that is in the future, still. Not a problem for this day.

She holds out to Mercedes the bunch of blue flowers: lupine, delphinium, penstemon. Her penance, her love. She opens the door.

ACKNOWLEDGEMENTS

"Virtue, Prudence, Courage" was published as "The Island" in *subTerrain Magazine* 8.78 (2018).

"Clearwater" was published in *Prairie Fire* 38.2 (2017).

"Flowers of the Dry Interior" was published in *Prairie Fire* 37.3 (2016).

"Vagina Dentata" was published in *Room* Online, Winter 2016.

"The Burgess Shale" was published by CBC Canada Writes, CBC Website, 2012.

"The Canoe" was published in a chapbook by Okanagan College/UBC Okanagan, 2007.

"That Ersatz Thing" was published in *Geist* 14.56 (June 2005).

"Echolocation" was published in *Chatelaine*, November 1998.

I acknowledge the many hours of work donated by judges and juries of writing contests, especially the Okanagan Fiction Contest and *Prairie Fire* magazine. Thanks also to all of the editors who have loaned their sharp eyes for clarity and consistency, particularly Anne Nothof and Claire Kelly at NeWest Press. Susie Safford also gave helpful feedback to several of the stories in early drafts.

I am grateful to the office of Research and Graduate Studies at Thompson Rivers University for support in the form of sabbatical leaves.

Robert "Max" Metcalfe generously provided a paradise in which to write at his farm on the island of Öland in Sweden in the summer of 2014.

Many friends and family members have given me countless hours and kilometres of conversations and walks and that have inspired and shaped my fiction. I hope that my affection and appreciation will shine through any clumsiness in my efforts to create imaginative works.

KAREN HOFMANN grew up in the Okanagan Valley and is an Associate Professor at Thompson Rivers University in Kamloops, British Columbia. A first collection of poetry, *Water Strider*, was published by Frontenac House in 2008 and shortlisted for the Dorothy Livesay Prize. Her first novel, *After Alice*, was published by NeWest Press in 2014, and a second novel, *What is Going to Happen Next*, in 2017. Her short fiction has won the Okanagan Fiction Contest three times, and "The Burgess Shale" was shortlisted at the 2012 CBC Short Fiction Contest. Karen Hofmann is an avid walker, and her writing explores the landscapes, both rural and urban, of British Columbia as well as the personalities and social dynamics of the inhabitants.